NO PEACE UNTIL DEATH

Nate was taken unawares when Chevalier suddenly lunged and stabbed at his chest. He threw himself to the right, sweeping his knife up, and barely managed to deflect the thrust.

"I almost had you, Grizzly Killer," Pierre said cockily. "And we've only just begun."

"We can still lower our weapons and shake hands," Nate said.

"Never."

"Tell me, Chevalier. What happens if I should only wound you? Will you let bygones be bygones? Can we go our separate ways in peace?"

"You will never know peace as long as I'm alive!"

"That's what I was afraid you'd say."

The *Wilderness* series:

#12
WILDERNESS
APACHE BLOOD

David Thompson

LEISURE BOOKS NEW YORK CITY

A LEISURE BOOK®

June 2004

Published by

Dorchester Publishing Co., Inc.
200 Madison Avenue
New York, NY 10016

ISBN 0-8439-3374-7

The name "Leisure Books" and the stylized "L" with design are trademarks of Dorchester Publishing Co., Inc.

Printed in the United States of America.

Visit us on the web at www.dorchesterpub.com.

#12

WILDERNESS

APACHE BLOOD

Chapter One

They were only ten miles along on their journey when their huge black dog spied the hostiles.

It was late morning. The party of five, consisting of two brawny, bearded men, two lovely Indian women, and one grinning boy vibrant with excitement, had just crested a low ridge. Before them, extending from north to south, ran the long emerald line of rolling foothills that bordered the majestic Rocky Mountains to their rear.

In the lead rode a strapping young man sporting a mane of black hair that flowed past his broad shoulders. His alert green eyes swept the foothills and the well-nigh limitless prairie beyond, but he detected no movement. Satisfied, he started down the ridge, and it was then that the dog voiced a low growl.

Nathaniel King reined up sharply and glanced at the mongrel, which was gazing intently to the southwest, its thin lips curled up over its tapered teeth. "What's got you riled, Samson?" he asked softly, and stared in the same direction. Instantly he saw them, not quite a mile away, seven or eight riders moving between a pair of foothills, heading for the plain. He could tell they were Indians, but they were too far off to note details of dress and hair that would enable him to determine the tribe to which they belonged.

"Utes!" declared the white-haired man behind him. "A war party out to count coup, I reckon."

Nate snorted. "You're guessing, Shakespeare. You'd have to be an eagle to see them clearly from here."

The elderly mountain man gave a snort of his own. "That's the trouble with you young cubs. Your don't use your senses—your eyes, ears, and nose—like you should, the way animals do. That's because your brains are always half asleep," he said, and launched into a quote from his favorite playwright. "Care keeps his watch in every old man's eye, and where care lodges, sleep will never lie. But where unbruised youth with unstuffed brain doth couch his limbs, there golden sleep doth reign."

Despite himself, Nate chuckled. His mentor's passion for the writings of William Shakespeare was legendary among the trapping fraternity, which explained the nickname bestowed on McNair years ago by his friends. "If you say they're Utes, I'll believe you," he responded. "You're seldom wrong."

"What do you mean by *seldom*?" McNair demanded.

Nate was watching the band below. Utes often attacked whites on sight, and he had to be ready to get his family to safety. Fortunately, the warriors were moving to the east, their backs to the ridge. Unless one of them turned completely around, he and his loved ones were safe. Even so, his left hand gripped the Hawken resting across his thighs a bit tighter.

Like most free trappers, Nate was a walking arsenal. In addition to the rifle, he carried a pair of single-shot

.55-caliber flintlocks tucked under his wide brown leather belt. On his right hip, in a beaded sheath, was a large hunting knife. Wedged under his belt above his left hip was a tomahawk. And slanted across his powerful chest was a powder horn and an ammo pouch.

"Should we take cover, Pa?" inquired the boy, seated astride his roan a few yards from McNair.

"No, Zach," answered Nate. "We hold still until they're gone. Remember what I taught you about how much easier it is to see something that's moving than something that's not?"

"Yep," Zachary said. "And I've been practicing, Pa. The other day an old she-bear walked right by me and didn't bat an eye. She figured I was a tree or a bush, I bet!"

"Oh? I thought I told you to stay away from bears. Grizzlies will tear you to pieces, boy. And even black bears can be mean when—"

"The Utes," Shakespeare interrupted urgently.

One look showed Nate why. The band had stopped for some reason, and the last several warriors were still visible in the gap between the hills.

Suddenly the warrior bringing up the rear stretched and idly surveyed the surrounding countryside. He scanned both hills, then twisted to admire the snow-crowned Rockies.

"Keep your horses still," Nate cautioned the others, and hoped the swishing of their animals' tails wouldn't give them away. There was no way to stop their mounts and the four packhorses from moving their tails. But at such a distance, the odds of the Ute noticing were slim. It would take someone with sharper eyes than McNair to spot such slight motion.

His own horse, a superb gelding distinguished by black leopard spots on a dusky background, was holding itself as rigid as a statue. Pegasus was the name he had given it, in remembrance of a mythical flying steed he had often read about as a child. The gelding was a gift from the grateful Nez Percé, bestowed after he helped them fight off a Blackfoot war party.

Few white men owned a Nez Percé horse, although most would give a year's wages to do so. This was because the Nez Percé had been breeding their Palouses, as the breed was commonly called, ever since the days of the Spanish conquistadors. Now, few horses could match a Palouse for speed and endurance. They were highly prized by all men who knew their horseflesh.

Pegasus, in fact, had been the object of much envy from Nate's fellow trappers at the annual Rendezvous. Some had made generous offers to buy him, but Nate had refused them all. Pegasus was the best horse he'd ever owned—the best he had ever seen—and he would rather part with an arm or a leg than the gelding.

So now, as the Palouse stood stock still as if sensing their danger, he affectionately touched his hand to its neck and whispered, "Good boy!" He saw the Ute warrior face front again, and moments later the band vanished into dense forest.

"Do you reckon that one saw us?" Zachary asked.

"I don't rightly know," Nate said uncertainly.

Shakespeare voiced his thoughts. "If he did, he wouldn't let on. He'd wait until they were out of sight, then tell the rest. And as sure as shootin', they'd decide to shadow us and ambush us when we least expect it."

"Maybe you're wrong," Zach said with the typical optimism of the very young. "Maybe all they'd want to do is trade. We have plenty of supplies we can do without."

"Trust me," Shakespeare said. "They wouldn't settle for a few fixin's when so much more could be theirs for the taking."

"Like the horses and stuff?"

"And stuff," Shakespeare replied grimly.

The mountain man's underlying meaning was plain to Nate, who studiously avoided glancing at the two women behind his son. Both his wife and Shakespeare's made no comment, but he knew they both understood. Both had lived all their lives in the Rocky Mountain region; both were fully aware of the harsh realities of life in the savage wilderness.

He tapped his heels on Pegasus's flanks and began the descent. After going ten yards he looked back and smiled at Winona, the Shoshone beauty who had claimed his heart the very first time he ever laid eyes on her, although he had been too stubborn to admit as much for a short while thereafter. She had on an attractive buffalo hide dress she had made herself, as she had all of the family's clothing. Her raven hair, which hung past her hips when she was standing, swayed with every stride her mare took.

"I do declare!" Shakespeare said with a grin. "You are the darnedest one for making cow eyes that I ever did see!"

"And you never do?" Nate retorted.

"Not on your life. A growed man like me has too much dignity for such tomfoolishness."

Light laughter burst from the lips of the woman riding beside Winona. Blue Water Woman, a full-blooded Flathead, was more than twice as old as Nate's wife but hardly showed her age. A few streaks of gray in her hair and small telltale wrinkles at the corners of her lively eyes were the only evidence of her added years. She pointed at McNair, then said in slightly accented English, "If I was given a prime beaver pelt every time you bend the truth, husband, I would have more than have been caught by all the trappers who ever lived."

"He makes cow eyes too?" Nate asked, enjoying the slight crimson tinge on his friend's full cheeks.

"I tell you, Nate," Blue Water Woman said. "One of the reasons I became his wife is because he makes better cow eyes than any man I have known."

"Women!" Shakespeare muttered. "They are all but stomachs and we all but food. They eat us hungerly, and when they are full they belch us."

Unfazed, Blue Water Woman replied, "When it comes to belching, husband, you outdo a gorged buffalo."

Tickled by their banter, Nate grinned as he rode to the bottom of the ridge and swung to the southeast. It pleased him to see McNair bested. Blue Water Woman was one of the few people who could hold their own against Shakespeare in a battle of wits, which perhaps helped explain why they were so happy together.

Nate checked the gap once more. The Utes appeared to be long gone, but he wasn't taking any undue chances. For the next hour and a half he repeatedly searched for any sign of the band.

"I can hardly wait to get there," Zachary commented as they wound among the foothills toward the plain. "How long will it take us again?"

"That depends on a lot of things, young'un," Shakespeare said patiently, although the same question had been posed a half-dozen times since they left Nate's cabin. "It depends on how well the horses hold up, on the weather, on the water situation, and on whether we run into a lot of hostiles."

"Do you think we'll see Comanches?" Zach asked, fearfully accenting the last word.

"We might," Shakespeare said, "but I'm more worried about running into Apaches. They make the Comanches look like a ladies' sewing circle."

"They do? But Rafe Bodeen says the Comanches are the fiercest Indians this side of the Rockies. He says they can scalp a man so he never even notices his hair is missing.''

"Bodeen?" Shakespeare exclaimed. "Why, he's the biggest liar who ever donned britches. And what would he know about the Comanches anyway? He's never been south of Long's Peak."

"But he's heard tell all about them," Zach objected. "He told me so himself."

"Rafe Bodeen is a braggart who loves to hear himself jabber and to fill the heads of little boys with tall tales," Shakespeare said. "Why, if Rafe wasn't a human he'd be one of them there sperm whales."

"Tell me about the Apaches," Zachary prompted.

"Another time."

"Please, Uncle Shakespeare."

Nate looked over his shoulder and saw McNair's grizzled features soften. The mountain man liked being regarded as Zach's uncle, even though they weren't kin. And much to Nate's delight, Shakespeare enjoyed teaching Zach all the things a growing boy should know if he hoped to one day make a go of it in the mountains. Since Zach wasn't the only one who still had a lot to learn, Nate listened, engrossed, as the mountain man talked.

"The Apaches aren't like any tribe around. They keep to themselves high in the mountain country around Sante Fe and on down toward Mexico. Those who know say the Apaches have lived there forever, and none of the other tribes have been able to drive them out. Truth is, the other tribes are a mite scared of them."

"Even the Comanches?"

"Even the Comanches, though you'd have a dickens of a time making one own up to it. You see, Zach, the Apaches are warriors through and through. They love to go on raids to kill and plunder, and they're not too particular about who they raid. Whites, Mexicans, other Indians, it's all the same to them.'' Shakespeare paused and gazed thoughtfully at the remote horizon. "They're not at all like the Indians you know, the Shoshones and the Flatheads and the like, who organize war parties every now and then to teach their enemies a lesson or to steal horses. The Apaches live to make war and nothing else. They don't care much about buffalo hunting or fishing and whatnot. To them, war is everything.''

"Gosh,'' Zach said.

"Don't get me wrong, son,'' Shakespeare went on. "I regard them highly. In their own way, the Apaches are a noble bunch. They admire courage more than anything else. Which is why when they capture a man, they like to torture him. Not because they're more bloodthirsty than most. No, the torture is their way of measuring how brave a man is. If they think he's brave, they'll put him out of his misery quickly.''

"And if they don't figure he's brave?''

"Then they'll keep on doing what they're doing until he dies. They're not ones to show mercy to cowards.''

Zach had moved his roan closer to Shakespeare's white horse. "Have you ever seen an Apache up close?''

"Fairly close, once, more years back than I care to think about.''

"What happened?''

A shadow seemed to pass over the mountain man's face. "It was on my first trip to Santa Fe. Our caravan was camped a day shy of the town when some Apaches snuck into our camp and took one of the women, a wife of one of the traders. She screamed as they were hauling her off and we all ran to her rescue.''

Zach was practically glued to McNair. "Did you save her?''

The answer took a full five seconds in coming. "No, we didn't. Tried our hardest, mind you, but the devils had too much of a head start. We caught a few glimpses of them as they glided off like ghosts, but that was all.''

"And the lady?"

"I'd imagine she became the wife of an Apache warrior. She might even still be alive, though the odds are against it. White women don't take well to Indian living. They're too soft."

They rode in silence for a while, Nate pondering his friend's words and wondering if he had made a mistake in agreeing to this trip to Santa Fe. The journey had been Shakespeare's notion, the first lengthy break any of them had taken from their daily responsibilities since a similar trip to St. Louis a while back.

Ordinarily, the mere thought of the time and expense involved would have been enough to convince Nate to decline. But much to his surprise, Winona had expressed interest. And when Blue Water Woman also wanted to go, the die had been cast.

Perhaps, he reasoned, spring had something to do with it. The regal Rockies were aglow in the verdant splendor of springtime, with the tall trees and the high grass daily turning greener while the wild creatures resumed the active pace of their lives that had been disrupted by the bleak winter. After months of bitter cold and little food, the wildlife throbbed with vitality once again. The steep slopes echoed to the sharp cries of birds of prey and the strident calls of ravens and jays. Coyotes yipped on occasion, while at night the howls of wolves wafted eerily on the wind.

Spring transformed the mountains from a barren domain of snow and stone into a lush paradise. The buffalo resumed feeding in great herds out in the open. Deer and elk were in abundance. Panthers prowled the thickets. Bears were ever in search of food, shuffling over hill and down dale. And a man had only to breathe in the cool, crisp, invigorating air to feel alive in the depths of his being.

The rekindling of life on such a grand scale was bound to have an effect on those who had been cooped up in their small cabins or lodges for months on end. Whites and Indians alike were eager to get out in the sun again, to hunt, fish, and frolic to their heart's content. Winona and Blue Water Woman were no exception. They'd longed for a break in their daily routine, and what better way than to take a trip to distant Santa Fe, a trip few Indian women ever got to make, a trip they could proudly tell their grandchildren about in the decades to come?

Nate was equally thrilled at the prospect of seeing new country and spending time in the leading center of the Mexican province of New Mexico. Santa Fe, he had been told, was founded by the Spanish way back in 1610, and since then it had grown and prospered remarkably well to where it now served as a focal point of trade between the United States and Mexico. Large caravans from the States regularly carried a wide variety of trade goods there. Trappers and mountain men frequently paid Santa Fe a visit to kick up their heels and squander their hard-earned money.

All of that was appealing, but Nate still had reservations. They would have to journey hundreds of miles through territory only Shakespeare had ever visited, and once south of Bent's Fort they ran the very great risk of encountering hostile bands of Kiowas, Comanches, or Apaches. The thought of them made him wish he had left his wife and son at home, but he knew trying to convince them to stay behind would have been a hopeless task. When Winona set her mind to something, she was as immovable as a giant boulder.

Nate was brought out of his reflection by another question from Zach.

"Uncle Shakespeare, what did you mean by white

women are soft? Do Ma and Blue Water Woman have harder skin 'cause they're outside a lot?''

Somehow McNair kept a straight face. ''No, Stalking Coyote,'' he said, using Zach's Shoshone name. ''White women are soft because, generally speaking, they're lazy. At least the well-to-do ones are. They'd rather have servants make their meals and mend their clothes and grow their vegetables than do it themselves. Instead of making their own dresses, they go to stores to buy the fanciest finery they can afford. When they need shoes, they buy them. When they need a new winter coat, they buy it.'' He sighed. ''They're pampered from cradle to grave, so it's no wonder they don't last long when they wind up in the hands of some warrior.''

''There must be something they can do right,'' Zach said.

''True. I reckon I'm being too finicky about their habits. They *do* know how to spend money better than most other folks.''

''Some of them are awful pretty. I saw some in St. Louis, remember?''

''That you did, but I figured you were too young to notice their eyelashes and such,'' Shakespeare said with a snicker.

''What's so funny?'' the boy asked.

''You take after your pa,'' Shakespeare replied, and quoted again, ''You are a lover. Borrow Cupid's wings and soar with them above a common bound.''

''What's that mean?''

''It means,'' Nate interjected, ''that your uncle better put a rein on that tongue of his before it gets him in deep trouble.''

''God shield I should disturb devotion,'' Shakespeare declared.

Zachary frowned. ''I'll be happy when I'm older so I can understand what you say.''

"Don't count on that, son," Nate told him. "I'm full-grown and half the time I don't have the slightest idea what he's babbling about."

"Babbling?" the mountain man blustered. "What fire is in mine ears? Can this be true? Stand I condemned for pride and scorn so much?"

Nate knew better than to debate the point when Shakespeare was in one of his infamous moods. McNair could quote the English bard at a drop of the hat and rant on for hours at a stretch if not cut short. As if to prove him right, Shakespeare pressed a hand to his chest in a perfect mimicry of a stage actor and commenced reciting some of his favorite lines.

"To be, or not to be. That is the question: Whether 'tis nobler in the mind to suffer the slings and arrows of outrageous fortune, or to take arms against a sea of troubles, and by opposing end them. To die, to—"

"Husband dearest," Blue Water Woman interrupted.

"Yes, my sweet dove?" McNair responded grandly.

"Much more of that and our horses will start dropping like flies. Maybe you should wait to entertain us until we stop for the night."

"Ouch. You've cut me to the quick, wench."

"Do you want me to make a salve of beaver oil and castoreum so you'll heal faster?"

The two women tittered.

"Do you see?" Shakespeare addressed Nate. "Do you see what happens when you teach your wife English too well? She turns on you like a rattler the first chance she gets."

Everyone was in such fine spirits that Nate temporarily forgot all about his concerns for their safety. He continued making for the edge of the prairie where the going would be easier, though they would be close enough to the forest-covered foothills to swiftly seek cover should hostiles appear. Beside Pegasus walked Samson.

He marveled again at the good fortune that had resulted in his becoming a free trapper. When he looked back at his past, at his one-time plan to be an accountant in New York City, he had to chuckle at his foolishness. If not for the many strange twists and turns his life had taken, he would still be there, spending his days seated at a desk instead of getting out and about, dealing each month with mountains of clerical work rather than admiring Nature's handiwork, dying a little more inside with the passing of each day, his soul withering away like a parched plant for lack of the things that mattered most in life.

A dense tract of undergrowth materialized on his right and Nate swung left to go around it. He absently peered into its depths, thinking he might spy a black-tailed deer he could shoot for their supper, but as his eyes roved over the tangle of branches and leaves he saw something else entirely, a massive dark shape that moved a few feet in his direction and then stopped. Alarmed it might be a bear, he reined up.

Suddenly the shape moved again, this time crashing through the brush in a twinkling and dashing out into the open where it halted to balefully glare at the intruders, its nostrils flaring, its short tail twitching.

Nate started to raise his Hawken, then thought better of the notion. A single ball seldom sufficed to drop a two-thousand-pound bull buffalo.

Chapter Two

Of all the wild creatures teeming in the untamed land between the mighty Mississippi River and the pounding surf of the Pacific Coast, none were larger or more formidable when provoked than adult buffaloes. Standing six feet high at the shoulders, with a horn spread of over three feet, buffaloes were capable of bowling over grizzlies, panthers, horses, or men with astonishing ease.

Normally buffaloes paid little attention to humans. A man could ride up close to a herd and watch them graze without fear of being charged. If concealed and upwind, a hunter might down any number of the shaggy brutes without the rest so much as batting an eye. But once the buffaloes realized what was happening, the peaceful herd became a rampaging horde of destructive behemoths.

Rare was the mountain man who came on a bull all by itself. Buffaloes were led by their instincts to gather together into herds of varying sizes. Now and then a cow with a newborn calf might be seen hurrying to catch up with the main body. But solitary bulls were an oddity.

Now, as Nate met the unwavering stare of the heavily breathing bull, he noticed that its coat lacked the usual healthy luster, that one of its horns had broken off near the tip, and that there was a wicked gash in its left rear leg exposing part of the bone. This was an old male, he realized, well past its prime. Perhaps it was ailing as well as injured. Whatever, it had fallen behind the herd to which it belonged and been unable to overtake them. So, all alone and perhaps sensing it would be at the mercy of the first hunters or wolves to come along, the bull had sought sanctuary in the thicket.

What would it do? Nate wondered, and shot a hasty glance at the others. They were all as motionless as he. Zach was wide-eyed. Shakespeare had a thumb on the hammer of his rifle but wasn't trying to bring the gun to bear. Samson, thankfully, was calmly staring at the bull.

Nate waited, tense with anticipation. About 15 yards separated Pegasus from the brute. At most he would be able to get off one shot if the monster attacked. The bull was sniffing the air while scrutinizing them, apparently undecided whether they were harmless or not. A few more seconds of silence, he thought, might convince it to turn and reenter the thicket.

Then Samson snarled.

The effect on the old bull was electrifying. It snorted, tossed its head, and broke into a lurching rush, lowering its head as it pounded straight at Pegasus.

In sheer reflex Nate snapped the Hawken to his shoulder, took a hurried bead, and fired. The blast was echoed by three others. For a moment it seemed as if thunder had peeled. The bull staggered, surged erect, and kept coming, and it was all Nate could do to wrench on the reins and get Pegasus out of the way. He saw the bison's good horn sweep past the gelding's side, missing by inches, and his right hand darted to a flintlock.

Already the bull was going after another victim, angling sharply at Shakespeare, whose white horse reacted with a frantic jump to the side that would have done justice to a pronghorn antelope. Again the bull missed, pivoted on its hoofs, and spied Zach.

The boy sat rooted in place, his mouth slack, his arms limp.

"Move!" Nate bellowed, aiming at the brute's ear. He cocked the hammer and squeezed off his shot just as the bull charged. To his left Shakespeare also fired a pistol.

At the twin retorts the buffalo stumbled, its legs scrambling for a purchase, and rose to its full height. Zach had collected his wits and was desperately striving to goad the roan into motion, but the panic-stricken mount refused to cooperate. Once more the bull closed, but much slower this time.

Nate moved to intercept the monster, intending to put Pegasus between the bull's horns and his son. As much as he loved the gelding, he loved his son more, and would gladly sacrifice the one for the other if there was no other choice.

Out of the corner of his eye he saw Winona galloping forward, her fingers flying as she shoved her ramrod home. She had the same idea he did, and she was nearer. His heart seemed to leap into his throat as she stopped in front of Zach and swept her rifle up. Exactly as he had taught her, she fixed the bead on the bull, cocked the gun, and fired, all in the span of a second. Her ball smacked home, loud enough for all to hear, and the next instant the brute was going down in a whirl of limbs and tail to slide several yards to a final rest almost at the very hoofs of her mare.

"Damn, that was close!" Shakespeare breathed.

Nate barely heard him. He was vaulting from the saddle and running up to the bull, which was down but not dead, its eyes fluttering and its sides heaving as it feebly struggled to stand yet again, the spark of life unwilling to relinquish its hold on the aged, torn hulk of a body. His second flintlock streaked clear. In a blur, he touched the barrel to the beast's side and sent a lead ball directly into its lungs.

Snorting in fury, the bull tilted its enormous head and took a swipe at the human gnat causing it so much pain. But its head had only swung a few inches when the bison abruptly stiffened, grunted, and collapsed, its tongue protruding from its mouth. Blood began dribbling from its black nose.

"That did it," Shakespeare commented.

Gulping air, Nate took a step backwards. His right hand was shaking uncontrollably. Inwardly he quaked at how close Winona had come to meeting her Maker. A glance into her eyes showed she was experiencing similar feelings. "Nice shooting," he remarked, and was shocked at his strained voice. He quickly coughed, licked his lips, and added, "I didn't know you could reload that fast."

"Nor did I," Winona said in such perfect English that anyone in the States who heard her speaking in the next room would have no idea she was a Shoshone. She had an exceptional gift for learning new tongues. Shakespeare, who had spent many years teaching not only Blue Water Woman but many other Indian friends the white's man language, had been amazed at how readily and thoroughly Winona learned it. She was, Shakespeare believed, a natural-born linguist. "I don't know how I did it," she mentioned.

"I do," Shakespeare declared. "Your blood was pumping like a geyser and you weren't thinking of anything but the safety of your young coon. I've seen folks do amazing things when their loved ones were in danger.'' He started reloading his rifle. ''Why, once I saw a Crow woman lift a tree that had been blown down during a storm and landed on her lodge, pinning her little girl. I was in a lodge across the way, and I ran right over with several warriors. The trunk of that tree must have weighed hundreds of pounds, yet she had it off the ground when we got there and we pulled her girl out. Later when she tried lifting the tree, she couldn't even budge it.''

Nate set to work reloading his own guns, glad to have something to do. Only a greenhorn left his weapons unloaded for longer than was absolutely necessary. In the wilderness a man never knew when danger might strike, as the attack of the bull buffalo had so vividly demonstrated. McNair himself had once put it best: ''An empty gun is the sure-fire sign of an empty head.''

Young Zach, who had not uttered a sound since the buffalo appeared, cast a tormented gaze at his father. ''I'm sorry, Pa. I truly am.''

''For what?''

''I'm yellow, Pa. I was scared clean through.'' Zach bowed his head in shame and added in Shoshone, ''My spirit is sick.''

Nate was in the act of pouring the proper amount of black powder down the Hawken barrel and he kept on pouring, only slower, giving himself time to think on how best to respond to his son's declaration. He had seen the fear on Zach's face, and he knew how upset the boy must be.

The matter wasn't to be taken lightly. Courage was one of the cardinal virtues of a Shoshone warrior, as young Zach was well aware. The driving ambition of every boy in the tribe was to one day prove his bravery in battle and then to be asked to join one of the prestigious warrior societies. Those who showed cowardice became social outcasts; they weren't permitted to share in many of the traditional activities of the men. Every boy acutely dreaded that happening to him.

"I've been scared quite a few times myself," Nate said, and smiled reassuringly at Zach. "Usually it's been when, like now, something happened so fast that I didn't have time to think. If, for instance, a grizzly should come charging at you from out of nowhere, you're first reaction is to run to another part of the country just as quick as you can go." He paused to cap the powder horn. "So being afraid every so often is perfectly normal, son. Don't let it get you down. There will be other times when you'll be put to the test and I know you'll do just fine."

"How do you know?" Zach inquired.

"I can answer that one," Shakespeare said cheerily, moving his mare over next to Zach. He gave the boy a hearty clap on the back and said, "You'll do fine because you're the son of Grizzly Killer, the man who has killed more grizzlies than any white man or Indian who ever lived. Never forget that some of your pa's blood flows in your veins, son. One day you'll be as well known as he is."

Under the mountain man's friendly influence, the boy brightened and nodded.

"I will, Uncle. One day I'll be as famous as Pa. No one will ever dare call me yellow."

McNair glanced at the bull. "Well, now we have to decide what to do about this critter. We already have enough jerked venison, pemmican, and other victuals to last us clear to Santa Fe. But we sure as blazes can't let this critter lie here and rot. I say we make camp here for a day or two and dry as much of the meat as we can, then tote it with us. Our pack animals can carry the extra weight with no problem."

"But why go to all that bother?" Nate asked, displeased by the delay it would cause. "Wolves, coyotes, and buzzards have to eat too."

"Wolves and coyotes didn't kill it. We did. That makes it our responsibility, as you well know," Shakespeare noted.

One of the cardinal unwritten rules of wilderness life was to never let good meat go to waste. Nate sighed and reluctantly nodded in agreement. "I reckon a day or two won't hurt."

Winona had dismounted and walked up to the bull. Reaching out, she placed a hand on the huge carcass and closed her eyes.

"Are you all right?" Nate asked, joining her.

She held still for a full ten seconds. Then she lowered her arm and gave him a look that radiated sheer love. "I was thanking the Great Mystery for the life of our son," she said softly so none of the others could hear.

He smiled and leaned closer to kiss her lightly on the cheek. Words were not needed. Their eyes eloquently conveyed their emotions.

"Now don't start with that cow-eyed business again," Shakespeare playfully chided them as he swung to the ground. "We'll never get this bull carved up with you two acting like you're courting."

Soon they were all busy at various tasks. Nate and Shakespeare rolled up their sleeves, pulled their butcher knives, and commenced removing the bull's hide, being careful not to tear it so later it could be made into a fine robe. Winona and Zach collected dry wood and built a small fire. Blue Water Woman took care of the horses, removing the saddles and packs and tethering the animals where they had plenty of grass to graze on.

Nate pondered as he worked. Here they were, barely started on their long journey, and already they were losing valuable time. He hoped it wasn't an omen of things to come. Then he reminded himself that he was viewing the matter as a white man would and not as an Indian. Whites, especially those living in New York and other cities back East, were always scurrying about like so many mice, always on the go, always trying to cram as many activities as they could into each day. They lived a hectic existence, rushing here and there and everywhere, Time their harsh taskmaster.

Indians, however, were vastly different in their outlook and way of life. They seldom rushed anywhere, unless it was to rush into battle should an enemy be sighted near their camp, or to rush off after buffalo if the village was in need of meat and a herd should be spotted nearby. Generally, though, Indians went about their daily activities at a sedate pace, completing each chore properly and patiently before moving on to the next. When they ate their meals, they ate slowly. When they tanned hides, they took their time. When a horse needed breaking, it was done over a period of days, not hours. In almost all things Indians did, they worked at a relaxed pace. The precious moments of each day were savored, not gulped at a single draught. Time was of no consequence in this regard, and as a result they were the masters of Time and not the other way around.

This train of thought made Nate realize how foolish his annoyance had been, and he consciously willed himself to relax and enjoy the interlude. He even whistled as he sliced away, and suddenly he was conscious of being watched.

"What, pray tell, has put you in such fine fettle?" Shakespeare wanted to know. "A while ago you were acting as if you had a burr up your backside."

"It feels good to be alive," Nate said simply.

"That it does," Shakespeare concurred. "As there comes light from heaven and words from breath, as there is sense in truth and truth in virtue, that it does."

"More William S.?"

"Of a sort."

It took them well into the afternoon to butcher the bull

to their satisfaction. By then Winona and Blue Water Woman had set up a crude framework of trimmed branches on which to hang the thin strips of meat. Everyone pitched in to help, and soon the job was done.

Five thick, juicy masses of prime bull meat were saved for supper, and so toward sunset the two women unpacked their cooking utensils, both owning a number of tin pans, cups, plates, and whatnot obtained at a previous Rendezvous, and started cooking the meal. Winona dug out her coffeepot, and was walking to the fire when she stopped and glanced at Nate.

"Have you seen Zach?"

Nate looked in all directions, but the boy was gone. He recalled seeing Zach and Samson heading into the forest to the north of their camp shortly after the meat was hung out to dry, but he'd thought nothing of it at the time. Boys loved to go exploring, and Zach was no exception. Grabbing his rifle from where it rested on his saddle, Nate hiked toward the tree line. Zach knew enough not to stray far, and Nate was confident he would find his son quickly.

At the edge of the trees he came on their tracks and followed them into the pines. True to form, the boy had wandered from one attraction to another, first a partially rotted log, next a tree that had been struck by lightning, and so on, meandering ever deeper into the solitude of the woodland. At length Nate spied a hill ahead. Sure enough the trail led him to its base. Above him, scattered about the slope, reared dozens of large boulders, some bigger than his cabin.

"Zach?" Nate called.

There was no answer.

"Zachary!" Nate yelled. Once more no reply was forthcoming, and he became irritated that the boy had strayed off much farther than was wise. He cupped a hand to his mouth to try a third time. "Zachary King!"

From somewhere near the top of the hill came a sharp yip.

"Samson?" Nate said, and began ascending. He heard a louder bark. Going around a boulder, he saw the great black dog standing 40 yards away near what appeared to be a rock ledge.

"There you are. But where's Zach?"

Concerned, Nate hurried. Samson barked several times, as if urging him on. When he was still ten feet off the dog whirled and dashed onto the ledge, then turned and barked again. "What's got you so worked up?" Nate asked.

The ledge turned out to not be a ledge at all, but rather a spot where long ago the ground had buckled and cracked, creating a narrow fissure that extended deep down into the earth. On either side of the fissure was a shelf wide enough for a person to stand on. Nate stood on the rim and scanned the top of the hill. "Zach? Where are you?"

"Down here, Pa!"

The muffled response, coming as it did from under Nate's very feet, made him stiffen in shock, then drop to one knee. He could see 20 feet down into the fissure but no further. Beyond that the sunlight didn't penetrate. "Zach? Are you hurt? What happened?"

"I'm scraped up some," was the answer. "I was trying to see what's at the bottom and I slipped."

The opposite wall was as smooth as glass, the near wall rough and laced with cracks. "Can you climb back out?" Nate inquired, trying not to betray his anxiety. He had never liked enclosed spaces, and the thought of his son trapped down there gave him the jitters.

"No. I've tried, Pa, but my left leg is stuck."

Nate's mind raced. He could climb down himself, although it would be a tight squeeze, but what if he also became wedged fast? "You hang on, son. I'm going back to the camp for some rope and some help. I'll be back before you know it."

"Okay, Pa."

"I'm leaving Samson here so you'll have some company."

"Hurry, please. I'm afraid my leg will slip free and I'll fall the rest of the way."

"You're not at the bottom?"

"No, sir. I think the bottom is a long ways down yet. I dropped a stone but I didn't hear it hit."

"You just hang on," Nate reiterated, rising. He motioned at Samson to stay, then whirled and went down that hill as if he had wings on his feet. Horrifying images of Zach plunging into the depths of the fissure lent speed to his legs. When he burst from the trees the others were gathered around the fire, sipping coffee. They had only to take one look at him to shove to their feet in apprehension.

"What is it?" Shakespeare asked.

Nate told them as he rummaged in the packs and located the length of rope he always included in his supplies. Spinning, he started back and the three of them fell in alongside him. He glanced at Winona, about to tell her that someone should stay with the horses and their provisions. The set of her features changed his mind. She had just as much right to be there as he did.

It seemed to him that they were moving at a snail's pace. Since he was the fleetest of foot, he swiftly pulled out ahead, weaving among the pines and vaulting all obstacles with ease. The hill broke into view and he raced upward, the soles of his moccasins digging into the soil for a firm purchase. Samson, obediently, had not budged.

"Zach?" Nate shouted.

"I'm here, Pa."

"I've got some rope. I'll be down there in no time," Nate said, and scoured the shelf for a projecting rock or an adequate boulder to which he could secure the rope. There were none. The nearest boulder was five feet below the fissure on the right. Dashing over, he made a loop, and was tying it when Shakespeare, Winona, and Blue Water Woman reached the shelf.

"Tarnation!" Shakespeare exclaimed. "How the devil did he manage to fall in there?"

Nate was too busy to reply. Once the rope was attached, he moved back to the rim and handed his Hawken to Winona. "Keep an eye that the rope doesn't come loose," he cautioned.

She stared into the fissure. "Perhaps I should be the one to go down, husband. I am smaller than you."

"I can make it," Nate said, and stepped to the very edge. Balancing on his heels, he took up the slack and prepared to go over the side.

Shakespeare suddenly seized the rope to play it out slowly and gave a bob of his chin. "Don't fret none. I'll hold down this end. You just make damn certain you don't get yourself stuck or we might never get you out."

On that optimistic note Nate lowered his right leg down, then his left, bracing his feet against the inner wall. Gradually he eased lower and lower, straightening as he went, until his head was below the rim. He could feel the smooth wall brushing against his back and his heels. To say it was a tight fit was the understatement of the century.

He swallowed hard and kept inching downward. The close press of the walls jangled his nerves and set his teeth on edge. Waves of fear pounded at his brain but he refused to succumb. That was his son down there, and he would do whatever was required to save the boy, just as would most any other Shoshone or white father. Parents since time immemorial had been laying down their lives to protect their offspring. Such caring self-sacrifice was one of the most basic of human instincts in those who had not fallen into the mistake of loving themselves more than they did their own children.

"Zach?" he called to get his bearings as he sank into the gloom below.

"Over here, Pa."

Nate peered to his left, waiting for his eyes to adjust to the dark, and worked his way ever lower. A minute later he spied Zach's upturned grimy face lined with worry. Grinning, he said casually, "You beat all sometimes, son. I swear I'm going to start putting a leash on you so you won't wander farther than you should." He expected Zach to laugh. Instead, the boy frowned.

"Be real careful, Pa. I think I heard something earlier."

"What?"

"Something was moving around."

"All the way down here? You're loco," Nate joked, and then froze because he heard something himself, a slight scraping noise to his right. He looked, and barely made out the outline of a ledge that couldn't have been more than three or four inches wide, which wasn't very wide at all, but still more than wide enough for the large rattlesnake that was slowly crawling toward him.

Chapter Three

How the snake got down into the fissure hardly mattered. The sight of its distinctive large triangular head and its thick body patterned on the back with dark diamonds bordered by a lighter shade sent a chill rippling through Nate. He imagined he could see the snake's markings clearly, but of course he couldn't in the shadowy confines of the crack. He did hear the sibilant hiss of its flicking tongue and a faint rattle as its tail moved along the thin ledge.

"Pa?" Zach asked, having sensed that something was wrong.

Nate made no reply. With a start he realized the thin strip of stone on which the snake was crawling ran right past his face, angling upward toward the rim. Holding himself rigid, his breath catching in his throat, he watched the reptile glide closer.

"Pa? What is it?"

The rattler, head held low, drew abreast of Nate, and

he could see its slender tongue testing the air. Its eerie eyes were fixed straight ahead, its scales rippling as it climbed. He kept waiting for the deadly serpent to crawl out of sight so he could relax.

Unexpectedly, just then, with the fine particles of dust suspended in the air, Nate felt an urge to sneeze. The impulse was nearly overwhelming. Yet he dared not let go of the rope to clamp his nose shut or his forearm would brush against the rattlesnake. Nor dared he sneeze, for the rattler might turn on him in the blink of an eye and strike.

In despair Nate bit down hard on his lower lip, his teeth digging deep into his skin. Intense pain seared through him, pain he hoped would suffice to take his mind off sneezing. The tingling in his nose slacked off for a few seconds, which was all the time needed for the rattlesnake to slide into the darkness and be gone.

Unable to control himself any longer, Nate sneezed so loud that more dust swirled off the wall and enveloped his face. He began coughing, which caused the rope to shake violently, and his sweaty hands started to slip. Girding his muscles, he held fast until he could inhale without difficulty.

"Pa?" Zach said, sounding greatly concerned.

"I'm fine," Nate answered. "Just saw a snake." He resumed lowering himself down. Reflecting on the close call, he realized there might be many more rattlers in the fissure. Some snakes liked to hole up in cool, quiet places during the heat of the day. Sometimes hundreds or even thousands congregated in a single den. It was possible there were hordes of rattlers somewhere at the bottom, and he worried what would happen if either of them should plummet into the fissure's depths.

"My left leg is falling asleep," Zach remarked.

Yet another worry, Nate thought, scowling. If the boy's circulation was being cut off, there might be internal damage to the leg. He shifted so he could slide down next to his son, and tensed his left arm to bear all of his weight as he tried to squeeze his right arm around Zach. Nothing doing. The walls narrowed at the very spot where Zach was stuck, and it was well they did. On either side was a bit more space, enough so that the boy would have plunged all the way to the bottom had he missed that spot by a matter of inches either way.

"I'm sorry, Pa," Zach said softly.

"We all have accidents from time to time," Nate said, and let it go at that. Which struck him as ironic. If he had pulled a harebrained stunt like this on his own father, he would have received a tongue-lashing to beat all tongue-lashings and a whipping that would have left him unable to comfortably sit down for a month. And, truth to tell, if he had never left New York, if he had married someone there and raised a different family, he would probably have acted the same way if his son did something similar.

But living with the Shoshones had changed him. Living as an Indian had altered his perspective on life. Indian parents rarely resorted to physical punishment. Stern words, yes, and discipline that involved extra work or the denial of favorite pastimes, but not spankings or slappings or beatings with a rod. Indian parents regarded incidents like this one as educational. The only way for a child to learn, they believed, was for that child to go out and experience life. If the child committed a foolish act, then the child suffered the consequences and learned never to be so foolish again. Certainly there were risks in allowing children to learn so much for themselves, but the gains outweighed the risks, the gains being that Indian children matured more quickly than their white counterparts, acquiring a practical wisdom that stood them in excellent stead the rest of their lives.

Nate eased lower and attempted to get his arm around

Zach's legs. There wasn't enough extra room for a finger, let alone his whole arm. Frustrated, he went even lower until he was below his son. Bracing his back against the rear wall for extra support, he put his right palm against the sole of Zach's left moccasin and pushed.

"Ow!" the boy cried out.

"This will likely hurt a bit," Nate said, "but it can't be helped." Once more he pushed, and felt the wedged leg give slightly.

"Don't fret about me, Pa," Zach said through clenched teeth. "Do what you have to."

Pride swelled Nate's heart. He pushed harder, working the foot back and forth as much as he was able, and gradually the leg loosened. Dust cascaded onto his face, forcing him to avert his gaze. His left shoulder and his back were hurting, but he paid them no heed. Patiently he continued moving his son's foot until the leg abruptly slipped free to one side.

Instantly Zach, who had been clinging to the wall with clawed fingers, started to slid down. Nate lunged upward, looping his right arm about Zach's waist, and arrested the fall. "Hang on tight," he advised. Then, hugging his son close, he commenced his ascent.

"We're coming out!" he yelled.

The rope leaped upward of its own accord, hauling him toward the welcome light overhead at twice the speed he could manage on his own. Once or twice his back bumped the wall, and once his elbows were jarred, but the discomfort was a small price to pay for being swiftly pulled to the surface. There he found not only Shakespeare but also Winona and Blue Water Woman had helped to get him out.

"Thanks," Nate said, rising to his knees and lifting Zach upright. There were tears of gratitude in the boy's eyes.

"I won't ever do anything like that again, Pa. I promise."

"Let's hope not," Nate said. "I'd rather wrestle a grizzly than be hemmed in like a pea in a pod."

Winona stepped up and gave Zach a hug; then she examined his left leg. The boy's leggin was torn and his skin scraped badly, but there was scant blood and the bone was unbroken. The only comment she made while conducting her examination was, "You must remember to be more careful in the future, my son. Sometimes I think you are as accident-prone as your father."

In the act of rising, Nate had opened his mouth to deliver a witty retort when he saw Samson standing with head held high and ears erect, staring in the direction of their camp. He twisted, gazing out over the trees, and saw the thin spiral of smoke that indicated the location of their fire. He also heard, faintly on the wind, a series of high-pitched whinnies.

"Something is in our camp!" Shakespeare bellowed, and was off the shelf like a shot, sprinting down the slope with great leaps, a human bighorn in action.

"Bring the rope!" Nate said, and followed his mentor, scooping up the Hawken first. At the base of the hill he could hear the agitated horses clearly, and he prayed a panther wasn't after them. Or worse, a grizzly. The loss of a pack animal wouldn't be so bad, but if one of their mounts should be ripped apart they would be forced to turn around and head home.

A glance back showed Winona and Blue Water Woman trying to undo the knots he had made when he tied the rope to the boulder. Good, he reflected. They would be delayed getting to the camp, which should give Shakespeare and him time to deal with whatever was spooking the horses before they got there.

For an old-timer, McNair was incredibly spry when

he had to be. Ten yards ahead he darted around an ever-green and jumped over a log.

Nate willed himself to catch up. If a wandering grizzly had struck their camp, it would take both of their rifles to bring the monster down. Single shots hardly ever did the trick. More often than not, a grizzly would be shot seven, eight, nine times and still keep coming, its lungs perforated and its innards shot all to hell, yet still able to tear a man to shreds with a single swipe of its mighty paw.

He glimpsed the end of the trees at the same moment he drew even with McNair. Past the pines on the right were the tethered horses, some prancing in place as if their hoofs were on fire.

"I hope it's not those Utes," Shakespeare said.

That hadn't occurred to Nate. The band was in the area, though, and might have spotted the smoke, a care-less oversight on their part that never would have hap-pened if they hadn't become distracted by Zach's plight. He lifted the Hawken, ready for a bloody battle, and charged from cover.

Standing next to the rack of drying buffalo strips was the intruder.

Nate and Shakespeare dug in their heels and halted side by side. A whiff of rank odor hit Nate a second later and he scrunched up his nose. His thumb on the hammer uncoiled. Under no circumstances would he shoot, and risk having to take two or three baths a day for six months to erase the even worse foul smell that would ensue.

Sniffing daintily at the meat, a large skunk walked slowly around the rack, then ambled close to the fire. The flames weren't to its liking, so it shuffled toward the horses. Several tried to pull their picket pins out in their efforts to get away from the brazen creature. Others shook their heads and snorted. The skunk, oblivious to the commotion it was so innocently causing, again changed course, moving toward the forest.

Nate's eyes widened as he saw it coming his way. Should he run or stay still? He heard Shakespeare whisper to stand fast, so he did. The skunk paused to paw at the earth briefly, then resumed its evening stroll. Suddenly it caught their scent and halted.

Ordinarily a skunk was no threat. Unless afflicted with rabies, skunks either gave humans a wide berth or ignored them entirely. And while nocturnal by nature, they were not averse to coming out before sunset when the whim struck, as this one had done.

Nate could see its dark eyes swiveling from Shakespeare to him and back again. What was it thinking? he wondered, watching it closely. There was no evidence of the telltale ring of drooling saliva common to animals with hydrophobia, so his only worry was the oily, fetid musk contained in glands in the animal's backside. A grown skunk could spray ten to 15 feet with astounding accuracy. Often it went for the eyes, since the musk would blind anyone or anything long enough for it to get away. Many an unwary Indian and trapper had found out the hard way just why the lowly skunk was shunned by fierce panthers and savage grizzlies alike.

Seconds passed. The skunk didn't move.

Then there was a crashing in the brush and a black form hurtled into the open and stopped between Nate and Shakespeare. Samson no sooner saw the intruder than he lowered his hairy head and vented a warning growl that would have scared any other creature half to death.

Not so the skunk. It chattered like an irate squirrel, stamped its small front paws, raised its hind legs, and arched its bushy tail.

"Move!" Shakespeare shouted.

No prompting was needed. Nate dived to his left,

springing as far as he could go. Over his shoulder he saw
Samson take a step, and he started to yell, to tell the dog
to sit, to stay, but he was too late. The skunk had already
spun. From its rear end shot a jet of vile liquid that
splashed squarely onto Samson's brow.

The dog recoiled, blinked, and snorted. Backing away,
Samson frantically rubbed a paw across his nose, then
rubbed his forehead on the grass. Neither helped. Turning, he vigorously shook his head and wheezed while
staggering a few feet.

Prone on the ground, Nate faced the skunk. A healthy
one was capable of unleashing five or six shots of musk
in swift succession, and he had no desire to be its next
target. The intruder, however, had no further interest in
them. It was walking to the west with the peculiar rolling
gait common to its breed, head and tail held proudly on
high, not the least bit concerned about reprisals.

"Damned arrogant critter!" Shakespeare muttered.
"Why the Good Lord saw fit to make them, I'll never
know."

"Maybe they're supposed to keep the rest of us hum-
ble," Nate quipped, and was immediately sorry he had
spoken because he inhaled a few stray tendrils of musk
lingering in the air. Coughing and gagging, he stood
and moved farther from Samson. The hapless mongrel,
meanwhile, had fallen to the ground and was rolling back
and forth in a frenzied bid to rid himself of the offending
stench.

"Want me to shoot it and put it out of its misery?"
Shakespeare asked, wearing a lopsided grin.

"Don't you dare!" yelped a shrill voice. Zach raced
out of the woods to crouch in front of the mongrel. "No
one harms my dog! Ever!"

"I was only joshing," Shakespeare said.

"You weren't funny," Zach declared, and tried to

stroke Samson's neck. The dog, ignoring him, wouldn't stop rolling. "Pa, what are we going to do?"

"Give him a good dunking in the first stream we find."

Zach leaned forward, his hand outstretched. "We can't . . ." he began, and gasped, his face contorting into a mask of utter revulsion. Doubling over, he covered his nose and mouth and hacked uncontrollably.

Nate took a breath, held it, and dashed to his son. Grabbing Zach around the waist, he carried the boy to the fire and gently set him down. "You'd better wait a spell before you try to pet him. He's not fit company for man or beast right at the moment." Looking up, he saw Winona and Blue Water Woman giving Samson a wide berth.

"What happened?" the latter asked, her eyes twinkling with inner mirth. "Don't tell us the famous Grizzly Killer was routed by a skunk."

"If word of this ever gets back to my people," Winona threw in, "Grizzly Killer will have to change his name to Smells Bad."

The two women laughed.

Knowing the futility of trying to respond to them, Nate walked to the horses and verified each was still firmly tethered. Next he checked the meat rack to see if any of the strips had been tampered with. All was in order. By the time he got back to the fire, Blue Water Woman was preparing fresh coffee and Winona sat with an arm draped on Zach's shoulders.

Shakespeare was trying to cheer the boy up. ". . . have days like this, son. Every one of us. It's the bad days that help us appreciate the good days more. Why, I remember one time your pa and me were out trapping beaver. Danged if he didn't get himself attacked by a black bear, a grizzly, and a Ute, all on the same day."

"At least I didn't get myself caught by a Blackfoot war party like someone I could mention," Nate interjected.

"Who?" Zach asked.

Shakespeare coughed and quickly went on. "That's not important. What matters is that you don't let a little accident now and then get you down in the doldrums." He rested a hand on the boy's arm. "This is in thee a nature but infected, a poor unmanly melancholy sprung from change of fortune."

"What?"

Sadly shaking his head, Nate squatted and picked up a tin cup. "I do wish you'd use common English with him, Shakespeare. He never understands when you warble like the bard."

"Warbling, is it now?" the mountain man responded a bit testily. He quoted from another play. "When a man's verses cannot be understood, nor a man's good wit seconded with the forward child, understanding, it strikes a man more dead than a great reckoning in a little room. Truly, I would the gods had made thee poetical."

Nate shrugged. "I never was one much for rhyme and all that. Give me a Cooper novel any day and I'm content."

"James Fenimore Cooper," Shakespeare spat, and reverted to the trapper vernacular. "That long-winded varmint! He's more in love with words than he is with life. Old William S., on the other hand, was a man who knew people. Knew the way they think, knew the way they act. He saw right through them and wrote the truth. Cooper? He's a literary flash in the pan compared to William S."

"I've read all of Cooper's books and I don't recollect coming across a lie in any of them," Nate countered. As with many of the free trappers, reading was one of his favorite pastimes, especially during the long winter months when the cold and the snow drove everyone indoors. A good book helped pass the hours pleasurably. Naturally, every trapper had an author he liked more than other writers, and heated arguments over the merits of each often arose. Some, like McNair, were partial to Shakespeare, although none had gone to the trouble he had to memorize all of a dozen plays. Some preferred Byron, some Scott. A few would read the Bible and nothing else. Nate often thought that many of the good citizens back in the States, who tended to view trappers as illiterate savages little better than the Indians those citizens despised so much, would have been shocked to learn the truth.

Leaning back against his saddle, he sipped his coffee and contentedly watched Winona and Zach talking in low tones. The boy was happier, and under Winona's influence he would soon be his old indomitable self. Children were like that. They bounced back from hard times faster than adults, maybe because they weren't so set in their ways and could take things more in stride. Children were like saplings, bending whichever way the wind blew but seldom breaking. Adults were like trees in their prime, able to bend, but more likely to snap if the wind blew too strong.

He thought about the events of the day—the run-in with the old buffalo, the incident at the fissure, and lastly the encounter with the roving skunk—and grinned. Life in the wilderness was rarely dull. Seldom did a day go by when something unusual didn't occur. It was just one of many fascinating aspects about the wilderness that had so appealed to him when he first ventured west. Unlike city life, where a person suffocated under the drudgery of a daily routine, where each day was almost an exact duplicate of the one before, life in the Rockies was an unending series of adventures big and small. A person felt *alive* in the wild.

Shakespeare, who had been gazing to the south while

drinking coffee, now stood and came around to Nate and knelt.

"Come to declare a truce?" Nate asked, and grinned.

"No," McNair said, shaking his head. He stared into the fire and spoke so quietly his lips barely moved. "Didn't it strike you as strange that our horses got so worked up over a skunk?"

"Not really," Nate said, wondering what his friend was getting at. "The critter must have wandered around the camp for a while before we got back. They didn't like its scent, is all."

"I thought so too until a minute ago," Shakespeare said. "Then I saw our other visitor."

"What other visitor?" Nate asked, sitting up so abruptly he spilled some coffee onto his lap.

"Take a gander at the trees south of us. Be casual about it so you don't spook him."

Placing the cup down, Nate stretched and shifted so he could scan the forest. He half expected to see a Ute lying in ambush, but for half a minute he saw no one. Then, as his brain sifted the random patterns of lengthening shadows and dying patches of sunlight, he saw a vague shape lying on the thick low limb of a spruce tree. It took a moment for the outline to become clear, and he whistled softly. "I'll be damned," he muttered.

"It must have been sneaking up on the horses when they picked up its scent," Shakespeare guessed. "It was the cause of the ruckus we heard when we were up on the hill. That skunk just happened to show up when we did."

"We can't let it sit there until dark," Nate said. "First chance it gets, it'll try for our stock."

"Do you want to do the honors or should I?"

"My rifle is handy," Nate said, picking up his Hawken. The women and Zach were watching him, puzzled. He cocked the hammer, then rose into a crouch. "Too bad we can't use any more meat," he mentioned.

"I know," Shakespeare said. "Panther meat is the best there is."

Nate pivoted on his heels, pressed the stock to his right shoulder, and aimed at the limb on which the powerful predator crouched. Steadying the barrel, he lightly touched the trigger, took a breath, and squeezed.

At the loud retort a tawny panther leaped clear of the limb and alighted on all fours in a crouch, its tail waving wildly, its ears flattened in anger. A feral snarl rumbled from its throat. For a moment it seemed about to attack, but the moment passed and the big cat spun and bounded into the forest, blending into the shadows with a skill not even the most seasoned Indian warrior could hope to match.

It all happened so rapidly that none of them got more than a glimpse of the magnificent animal. Nate slowly lowered his rifle and listened in vain for sounds of the creature's passage through the underbrush.

At length Zach laughed and said, "We sure are seeing a lot of critters on this trip. Maybe, if we're lucky, we'll see a grizzly soon."

"Bite your tongue, son," Nate said. "We're supposed to have fun on this trip, not fight for our lives every step of the way. I'll be happy if we don't tangle with anything else from here on out."

Little did he know what lay in store for them.

Chapter Four

Bent's Fort on the Arkansas River was actually a gigantic mud castle. There was nothing like it anywhere west of the Mississippi. Fort Union, situated where the Missouri and Yellowstone Rivers met, and Fort Pierre, on the northern Plains, were two of the bigger centers of the fur trade, but they could hardly hold a candle to the fort built by the Bent brothers and their good friend Ceran St. Vrain.

The front wall alone was 14 feet high, 137 feet long, and nearly four feet thick. The side walls ran for 178 feet. Huge towers had been constructed at the northwest and southeast corners, and each was constantly manned by alert guards who could effectively use the field pieces that had been brought in at much expense and with considerable hard labor to duly impress any and all hostiles.

Bent's Fort was an impregnable fortress. The whites knew it and could sleep soundly within its sheltering walls at night. The Indians also knew it, both the friendly tribes and the hostiles, so the latter didn't bother to waste the lives of their braves in trying to overrun it. The Comanches and Kiowas and others accepted its presence as inevitable, but many resented it all the same.

The fort almost qualified as a thriving colony. Up to two hundred men could be comfortably garrisoned there at one time, not to mention upwards of four hundred animals. Just inside the north and west walls were large corrals to accommodate the animals.

Nate had heard much about Bent's Fort, and was eagerly awaiting his first sight of the post. From a low rise he got his wish, and on spying the high adobe walls he broke into a smile. All of them did. He lifted his reins and started forward, but a word from Winona stopped him and he turned. "What's wrong?"

"Nothing, husband. Blue Water Woman and I must get ready."

"Get ready for what?"

"We must make ourselves presentable."

"You look fine to me," Nate said, and heard Shakespeare cackle as the two women rode off to be by themselves.

"For a married man, you sure have a lot to learn about womenfolk," the mountain man declared. "They're not about to wear their everyday dresses into the fort. It's fanfaron time, and there ain't a thing we can do but sit here and twiddle our thumbs until they're ready."

"What's fanfaron, Uncle Shakespeare?" Zach inquired.

"A French word, little one. Showing off, you might call it."

"What does Ma want to show off?"

"Ask me that question again in fifteen years and I'll tell you."

"Pa's right. You always talk in riddles."

"I try, boy. I try."

When the wives returned they had on their very finest ankle-length dresses made of the softest buckskin and gaily decorated with beads, fringe, and even a few tiny bells that jingled as they moved. They had plaited their hair and each wore a brightly colored ribbon; Winona's was red, Blue Water Woman's blue.

"My, oh, my!" Shakespeare exclaimed, doffing his beaver hat to them. "You beautiful ladies look fit for a Washington banquet. You'll be the talk of the fort."

"We would be pleased if it was so," Blue Water Woman said coyly.

Zach fidgeted in his saddle. "Can we go now? We've been waiting here for hours."

"It only seems that way," Nate mumbled, and assumed the lead. They had to swing around to the south side of the fort since the main entrance was located there. Along the way he saw a middling encampment of Indians close to the Arkansas River, 20 lodges arranged in a half-circle. "Arapahos?" he wondered aloud, knowing that tribe did extensive trading at the post.

"Cheyennes," Shakespeare answered.

Nate recalled hearing that it had been Cheyennes who had helped the Bents pick the site after William Bent had saved the lives of a pair of their warriors. Strategically placed at a crossroads of Indian travel, the fort now did a booming business with all of the tribes in the region. The Indians received guns, knives, tools, and trade trinkets in exchange for buffalo hides and other pelts. The Bent brothers and St. Vrain, all scrupulously honest, had acquired an unparalleled reputation for fairness so that even tribes who normally shunned the whites, such as the Gros Ventres and the Utes, routinely traveled to Bent's Fort to barter.

It had been several years since Nate last saw any Cheyennes. He had been meaning to seek out one of them for quite some time, a prominent warrior called White Eagle,

the man who had bestowed the name Grizzly Killer on
him after he slew his first monster bear by a sheer fluke.
That name had stuck, and now Nate was known far and
wide as the white who had slain more grizzlies than any
man alive. Not that he'd planned it that way. Somehow,
he seemed to attract grizzles the way a magnet attracted
iron. The truth be known, he would much rather attract
rabbits or squirrels.

The main gate was wide open, and both whites and
Indians were freely coming and going. Perched on the
wall above the gate was a belfry where a lookout sat. At
the first sign of hostiles he would sound the alarm and
rouse the entire garrison. This worthy now leaned forward to study their party. "Are my eyes playin' tricks
on me, or is that none other than Shakespeare McNair I
see?" he called out happily.

"Kendall?" the mountain man responded.

"None other," said the lookout, a strapping fellow in
a red cap. "I'm workin' for the Bents now, and finer
booshways you can't find anywhere."

"It's been a while," Shakespeare said. "How's the
family?"

"Lisa is as feisty as ever. And Vail is the apple of her
dear mother's eye. I'll introduce you later after my stint
here is done."

"I'll look for you."

They were about to pass through the gate when Nate
realized the nearest whites and Indians were looking his
way and some of the whites were scowling. He faced
straight ahead, acting as if he had no idea why they were
perturbed. Samson was certainly oblivious to their dirty
looks. He felt sorry for the mongrel because it still
smelled like day-old garbage after a dozen baths or better.

Once past the iron-sheathed gate, Nate gazed at a spacious inner court ringed by small whitewashed guest
rooms. Over to one side stood a well. There were also

offices, meeting rooms, warehouses, wagon sheds, rooms for the staff, and more, just as Shakespeare had detailed there would be. Although Nate had never set food inside the fort before, he felt as if he knew it as well as he did the interior of his own cabin.

There were Indians in abundance; Cheyennes and Arapahos and Osage and even a few Kiowas. Mingled among them were free trappers, Frenchmen from St. Louis, and voyageurs from far-off Canada. Altogether, it was as motley and colorful a gathering of humanity as anyone was likely to see anywhere west of the last Missouri settlement.

Nate made for a hitching post, running a gauntlet of frank stares. He began to dismount, then stopped in surprise on seeing a black woman emerge from a nearby doorway and scour the court for a moment before disappearing back inside.

Shakespeare grinned. "That's Charlotte, the cook. Stay on her good side, Nate, and you'll eat pumpkin pie and slapjacks as tasty as any offered in the fanciest home in New York City."

The ringing of a heavy hammer on an anvil drew Nate's attention to a blacksmith shop at the southeast corner of the fort, and when he turned back to the hitching post there stood a man with a receding hairline and aquiline features who was dressed in a fine black suit.

"As I live and breathe!" the man exclaimed, coming around the post and advancing on McNair with his hand extended. "Shakespeare, you old coon! What brings you to our neck of the woods?"

"Howdy, Bill," the mountain man said, swinging down and shaking heartily. "It has been a while, hasn't it?"

The man nodded. "I figured by now some Blackfoot would have your hair hanging in his lodge."

"I'm too ornery to let them get me," Shakespeare said. He proceeded to introduce Blue Water Woman, Winona, Zach, and finally Nate to the stranger. "This here is William Bent," he concluded.

"I'm delighted to make your acquaintance," Bent said. "Make yourselves at home here. If you're staying overnight, I'll arrange guest rooms for you."

"We'd be in your debt," Shakespeare said.

"Not at all. What are old friends for?" Bent responded, and moved off with a cheery wave.

"You didn't tell me that you knew one of the Bent brothers," Nate remarked.

"I know all three of them."

"Is there anyone you *don't* know?"

McNair, grinning, tied his horse to the post. "You have to remember that there aren't all that many white men in these parts. Sooner or later you'll meet most of them if you get around enough." He paused. "Bill and I go back to the time he was trading up in the Northwest. He was having a hard time making ends meet because of competition from the Hudson's Bay Company. There was many a time we'd sit around sharing whiskey and I'd listen to him describe his woes."

"Well, he doesn't have many woes now," Nate said, surveying the whirls of activity all around them. Here and there clusters of Indians were engaged in trade talks with members of the fort's crew. That the talks were effective was testified to by the enormous piles of prime pelts being prepared for transport by caravan to St. Louis, pelts easily worth several thousand dollars on the open market. The Bents and St. Vrain, he deduced, must be making money hand over fist. They'd soon be incredibly wealthy if they weren't already.

After Nate and Shakespeare assisted their wives down and secured all the animals, they all strolled around to

see the sights. Over Zach's protest Nate left Samson tied
with their horses. The dog whined and pawed at the rope,
but Nate refused to take the mongrel along and upset
everyone within sniffing distance.

They saw lusty free trappers drinking and laughing.
They saw proud Indians strutting about wearing new
blankets draped over their shoulders or adorned with new
trinkets. Toward the north end of the square, as they
completed their circuit, a peculiar series of subdued
cracking sounds could be heard. It gave Nate pause and
he scoured the square for the cause.

Shakespeare, who never missed a thing, pointed at the
roof of a building visible beyond the trader's room right
in front of them. "Billiards," he disclosed.

"Here?"

"Bill and his brothers have spared no expense in pro-
viding all the comforts. Do you play?"

"Of course. Every boy in New York City can play by
the time he's twelve. At one time I was rather good."

"Is that a fact? Then we'll have a match later. Our
wives should find it interesting."

"Say, Pa," Zach said, tugging on Nate's sleeve.
"What's that man doing to Samson?"

Turning, Nate beheld a trio of stern voyageurs ringing
the hitching post. A hefty specimen in buckskins and a
blue cap was angrily addressing Samson while jabbing a
thick finger within inches of the dog's face. Nate hurried
over, fearing trouble. Voyageurs were a hardy, indepen-
dent lot, as befitted men who made their living trapping
the most remote regions of Canada. Occasionally some
drifted south into the Rockies, but it was unusual for any
to be as far south as Bent's Fort.

"Is there a problem, gentlemen?" he politely inquired,
stopping close to the post.

The three scrutinized him from head to toe, their dark,
seamed features impassive.

"And who might you be?" demanded the one in the blue cap.

"I'm the man who owns this dog," Nate informed them. "Has he bothered you somehow?"

"You're damn straight he has, American."

"How?"

"Hell, take a breath," snapped Blue Cap. "The bastard stinks like dead fish." He spoke a sentence in French.

"I don't understand," Nate said.

"I asked if your dog is part skunk," the voyageur translated, his companions all smirking.

Nate struggled to control his surging temper. Voyageurs, he reminded himself, were renowned for their arrogance; they tended to look down their noses at their American counterparts, always acting as if they were better trappers and, therefore, better men. Better meaning tougher. All trappers took pride in being hardy souls. Voyageurs just went overboard.

"Maybe we should skin this ugly beast," the spokesman taunted.

"We can sell the meat to the Cheyennes," suggested another. "They love to eat dogs." Chortling softly, he bent over and reached for the mongrel's neck.

Samson wasn't about to let a stranger touch him. Bristling, he lunged, his great jaws snapping down on the Canadian's wrist, his teeth piercing the buckskin and digging deep into the man's flesh.

Shrieking in agony, the man threw himself backwards, tearing his arm loose and ripping his sleeve in the process. Large drops of blood dripped from the puncture marks. "Damn him!" he roared. "Look at what the son of a bitch did to me!"

The man in the blue cap, cursing a blue streak, drew a pistol and pointed it at Samson's head. "I'll teach this cur to mind its manners."

Everything transpired so quickly that there was no time for Nate to think, no time for him to do other than that which he now did—step in close and swat the pistol barrel aside with the stock of his Hawken. The flintlock discharged, the ball smacking harmlessly into the ground. "That will be enough!" he declared.

But the voyageur in the blue cap had other ideas. Enraged at Nate's interference, he suddenly sprang, swinging the pistol at Nate's forehead. Nate ducked under the blow and retaliated by driving the Hawken into the pit of the voyageur's stomach, doubling the man in half.

Strong arms abruptly clamped around Nate from behind, pinning him in place. "I've got him!" cried the other uninjured voyageur. "Bash his brains out, Pierre!"

Nate saw the one in the blue cap straighten and raise the flintlock overhead. Instinctively Nate lashed out, ramming his left foot into Pierre's knee. Pierre screeched and crumpled. The man who held Nate, roaring like a madman, drove forward, slamming Nate into the hitching post, and it felt as if a mule had kicked Nate in the gut. His lungs emptied in a great whoosh and he saw stars before his eyes. Dimly, he was aware the voyageur had drawn him backwards and was tensing to slam him into the post once more.

He mustn't let that happen! Twisting sharply, he succeeded in throwing the voyageur off balance. The man's arms slackened for a moment, and in that span Nate exerted all of his strength and wrenched himself free. Whirling, he glimpsed the voyageur clawing at the hilt of a butcher knife. Nate's fist stopped that, rocking the voyageur on his heels. A second blow dropped the unconscious Canadian in a heap.

Not until that moment did Nate hear the loud shouts on all sides and see men rushing from every direction. He backed next to Samson and held the Hawken level.

A few yards away was Shakespeare, covering the man Samson had bitten.

"What the devil is going on here?" asked an irate man with the bearing and dress of an aristocrat as he pushed his way through the crowd to the front. "Everyone knows the rules. No shooting is permitted in the fort. Nor will we tolerate fighting."

Shakespeare stepped up to Nate. "Don't lay an egg, Ceran. My friend Grizzly Killer didn't start the trouble." He bobbed his head at the Canadians. "They did."

"McNair?" said Ceran St. Vrain. "When did you get in?"

At that juncture William Bent hastened up from the other side and glared at the man named Pierre. "Shakespeare is telling the truth, Ceran. I happened to see what happened from the blacksmith shop." He jabbed a finger at Pierre. "You, Chevalier, have gone too far this time. You persist in imposing on our hospitality when we've warned you to behave."

"No one tells me what to do!" Pierre said, wincing as he cradled his knee with both hands.

"There you are wrong," Bent said calmly. "We will have your leg looked at, and then you and your friends will be escorted from the fort. Should you try to return, the lookout will be under my personal orders to shoot you on sight."

"You wouldn't dare!"

From out of the throng came Bent's employees, rugged Frenchmen and others armed with rifles, pistols, clubs, and knives. Fully a dozen strong, they stood on either side of William Bent, and all it took was one look at them for every man there, and particularly Pierre Chevalier, to realize they would gladly tear into anyone who in any manner threatened their employer.

"You were saying?" Bent said.

Pierre, his face beet-red, put both palms on the ground

and pushed upright. He tottered unsteadily for a bit, then shoved his pistol under his belt. "I'm not fool enough to stick my head into an open beaver trap," he said.

"You will gather your belongings and vacate the premises within the hour," Bent directed.

"If you insist," Pierre said bitterly. He glanced at Nate, hatred seeping from every pore. "This isn't over, Grizzly Killer. Not by a long shot. You will see my friends and me again soon. Very soon."

"Chevalier, why don't you do us all a favor and go jump in Lake Winnipeg?" Shakespeare asked.

The general laughter only further fouled Pierre's mood. "Have your fun, McNair. We'll be paying you a visit too. You had no call butting into this affair."

The crowd parted as the three Canadians were escorted into a nearby building, four fort employees carrying the one who was unconscious. With the excitement over, the rest of the gathering gradually dispersed.

William Bent and Ceran St. Vrain lingered.

"I wouldn't take Chevalier's words lightly, my friend," Bent told McNair. "He's not one to forgive a slight. He wears his hatred like most men wear clothes, and he can be as devious as a fox when he wants to be."

"I know all about him," Shakespeare said. "Don't worry. We'll be on our guard once we leave here."

"Which will be sooner than you expect if you are involved in any more disturbances," Ceran commented. "You always did have a knack for being in the thick of things."

"And you always did wear your britches too tight," the mountain man replied.

St. Vrain wasn't amused. "If you will excuse me," he said formally, and made for the building where the voyageurs were being tended to.

William Bent sighed. "You shouldn't have done that,

Shakespeare. I know the two of you never have gotten along very well, but he is my partner. I must put up with his stuffy attitude every damn day. Now I'll have to listen to him gripe about you for the next week or two.''

"Is that all? I'll have to insult him again before we go.''

"You're incorrigible," Bent said, turning. He inhaled deeply, then walked in a tight circle around Samson, examining the dog carefully. "Let me guess. He tangled with a skunk and lost. And you had the gall to inflict him on us?''

This last was addressed at Nate. "We couldn't very well leave him out on the prairie to fend for himself.''

"Why not?" Bent asked half seriously.

From between Winona and Blue Water Woman, both of whom had been standing quietly close at hand, stepped Zach. He ran up to Samson and affectionately threw his slender arms around the huge canine.

"Don't you worry, boy. I won't let anyone harm a hair on your head," he declared.

"There's your answer," Nate told Bent.

A warm smile curled the trader's mouth and he nodded knowingly. "I see your dilemma. Very well. The dog can stay, but you'll have to keep him in your room so as not to provoke another fight.''

"Fair enough.''

"Now come along and I'll show you where you'll be staying," Bent said.

The guest rooms, while small, were comfortably furnished. Most, they were informed, were currently empty, but that would soon change as the Bents were expecting a large caravan from Missouri any day now. During the spring and summer months an unending stream of wagons passed through en route to Santa Fe.

Bent stayed and chatted while they unsaddled. He lent

a hand in stripping their supplies off the pack animals, then graciously extended an invitation for them to join him and his wife for supper that evening.

Nate had only to see the spark of joy in Winona's eyes to accept. He walked outside with Bent and thanked him for the offer.

"My pleasure. It will make my dear wife happy. She so enjoys the company of other women." Bent stopped, glanced at the doorway, and lowered his voice. "I couldn't help but notice that both Winona and Blue Water Woman were carrying rifles earlier. It's most unusual to see women armed like that. Are they good shots?"

"The best. Shakespeare and I taught them ourselves. We figured it would come in handy if we're ever attacked by hostiles again. Four guns speak louder than two."

"Quite true. Wait until my wife hears." He took several strides, then cast a somber look of warning over his shoulder. "You might need four guns, my young friend, if Pierre and his bunch ever come looking for revenge."

Chapter Five

The large caravan from the States reached Bent's Fort the next morning a few hours after sunrise, and everyone turned out to see the heavily laden wagons arrive; trappers, mountain men, voyageurs, employees, and even the entire population of the Cheyenne village by the river.

Zach, perched on Nate's broad shoulders to get a better view over the heads of men in front of them, wiggled in glee and chattered constantly about the size of the wagons and the people he saw. This was a new experience to him and he enjoyed it with typical boyish zeal.

All the women at the fort, including Charlotte the cook, were splendidly dressed in their prettiest attire. Anyone unfamiliar with Indians ways would never suspect that the Indian wives of the free trappers, who stood so demurely by the sides of their spouses, were actually showing off. Gaily adorned in their finest buckskin dresses as they were, the wives were doing the exact same thing their wealthy white counterparts in high society did

when they donned expensive gowns to attend formal balls
and other social functions, proving once again that the
two cultures might be outwardly different, but that in
their hearts the two peoples were very much the same, a
fact few realized to the detriment of both.

There were 110 wagons in the wagon train and close
to two hundred men, traders and muleteers combined. All
were well armed. Caravans had to be strongly protected
against hostiles, most notably the wily Comanches and
the fierce Apaches.

At the head of the column rode two men, the wagon
boss and one other. William Becknell was the man in
charge, a veteran of the Santa Fe trade who was widely
hailed as "the Father of the Santa Fe Trail" because of
a shortcut he'd discovered some years back.

When trade between the States and Santa Fe commenced, the caravans left Independence, Missouri, and
struck off westward along the Arkansas River until they
reached the approximate spot where Bent's Fort would
later be built. From there they traveled southward along
the edge of the mountains, through Raton Pass, and then
eventually westward again until they hit Santa Fe. This
Mountain Route, as it became generally known, was long
and arduous.

Becknell had sought a shorter route. One year, instead
of following the traditional trail, he made a bold and
daring decision to leave the established route two-thirds
of the way to the cutoff to Raton Pass and strike directly
southwestward across the blistering Cimarron Desert. He
almost didn't make it. His party ran out of water, so to
survive they cut the ears of their mules and drank fresh
blood to quench their thirst.

This new route, the Cimmaron Cutoff as it was called,
shaved a hundred miles off the Mountain Route and became equally as popular with the traders. But there were
many who refused to take it. They were unwilling to

contend with the brain-baking heat, the roiling clouds of alkali dust that choked men and animals alike, and the deceptive mirages that led caravans off course. Then too, the Comanches were more apt to strike wagon trains taking the desert route than the mountain route.

So for years now both trails had been in regular use. The U.S. government helped out by paying two tribes, the Osage and Kansas Indians, who inhabited the central Plains, to leave the caravans alone, and by sometimes sending military escorts who would stay with the caravans until they reached Mexican territory.

This particular wagon train lacked a dragoon escort, Nate noted as he surveyed the line from one end to the other. He looked again at the man who rode beside Becknell, a dashing Mexican with a wide-brimmed white hat, a waist-length dark blue jacket that hugged his lean form, and matching blue pants that flared out at the bottom. Around the man's middle was a bright red sash, partially covering his white shirt. Tucked under that sash were two polished flintlocks.

"I've never seen his like before, Pa," Zach mentioned. "Is he from Santa Fe, you reckon?"

"He might be," Nate allowed.

"Gosh, he sure is a dandy."

"No more so than your mother," Nate recklessly joked, and received an elbow in the ribs for his wit.

Since the fort couldn't possibly hold so many wagons, the traders parked outside, dividing up into four groups and forming four protective circles. Afterward, they let their stock of mules, oxen, and horses loose to graze inside each ring, a standard precaution in case of an attack by hostiles.

Nate kept an eye on William Becknell during the activities. Bent had told him that Becknell invariably took the Cimarron Cutoff nowadays, but in this instance the wagon train was carrying a load of medical supplies, ammunition, and other provisions for the post, which necessitated taking the old Mountain Route.

Not being one to look a gift horse in the mouth, Nate waited until he saw Becknell and the Mexican dandy walking toward the iron gate. Then he excused himself, leaving Winona and Zach with Shakespeare, and moved to intercept the pair. Both halted at his approach.

"Mr. Becknell?" Nate said, offering his hand. "I'm Nate King, and I'm sorry to impose on you but I was wondering if my party can join your caravan to Santa Fe?"

The legendary wagon master scrutinized Nate from his beaver hat to his moccasins. "A mountain man is always welcome, sir. You're all fine shots and a few more guns might come in handy should the Comanches pay us a visit." Becknell admired the Hawken. "How many are in your party, Mr. King?"

Nate told him.

"Shakespeare McNair is with you?" Becknell said, sounding delighted. "Why, I haven't seen that old buzzard in seven or eight years. I should have known he'd be alive and kicking."

"You know him too?"

"Who doesn't? That man has a knack for getting around."

"Don't I know it," Nate said. "One of these days I expect I'll hear he's been to China and back."

Both Becknell and the Mexican laughed. The trader indicated his companion and said, "Where are my manners? Allow me to introduce a very good friend of mine, Francisco Gaona. His family is very prominent in New Mexico. He came north with me after my last trip to see some of the States for himself."

"My pleasure," Nate said, shaking hands. The Mexican's hand was firm, hinting at latent strength.

"Mine also, *señor,*" Francisco said, a hint of amusement in his eyes as he examined Nate's outfit. "Perhaps you would do me the honor of eating supper with us tonight? You are the first . . ." he paused ". . . mountain man I have met, and I would like to learn more about those who live as you do."

"My family would be glad to join you," Nate responded. He agreed to meet them at six o'clock, and promised Becknell he would bring McNair along.

The rest of the day was spent in mingling at the fort and with members of the caravan. Zach asked a million questions, wanting to know where the mammoth wagons were made and how much weight they could carry and why the front wheels were smaller than the rear wheels and why some wagons were pulled by mules while others were pulled by oxen, and on and on and on.

Nate answered as best he could, explaining that the wagons were made in Conestoga and Pittsburgh and other places, that each could carry up to ten tons of trade goods, that the front wheels were smaller so the wagons could make tight turns without difficulty, and that whether a man used mules or oxen was a matter of personal choice.

Shakespeare didn't help matters by snickering at some of the questions and suggesting some more for Zach to ask, such as why were mules so stubborn and were boy oxen stronger than girl oxen? McNair had no idea how close he came to being shot in the foot.

At the appointed hour Nate, his family, and the McNairs met Becknell, Gaona, and others from the caravan for a hot meal at the fort. They were joined by William Bent and Ceran St. Vrain. Charlotte outdid herself, treating them to succulent buffalo meat, biscuits, potatoes, beans, countless cups of rich coffee, and more.

It was after the meal, as they all sat around the long table chatting and, in the case of many of the men, smoking on their pipes, that an incident took place Nate never forgot for as long as he lived.

He was listening to Becknell talk about the unbelievable profits to be made in the Santa Fe trade. He heard how a recent caravan had transported $35,000 worth of goods there and returned to Missouri with $190,000 in gold, silver, and prime furs. It set him to thinking about how hard he had to work just to make ends meet, and how he was lucky if he made $2,000 dollars in any given year.

Preoccupied with his thoughts, he failed to notice the three men who crept in through a side door, until he heard the click of a gun hammer being pulled back and he gazed around in surprise to see the three voyageurs he had tangled with the day before not three yards away with their rifles trained on the group at the table.

Pierre Chevalier wagged his gun at Nate and smirked. "So we meet again, *mon ami*? But not as you would like, eh?"

Everyone was frozen in place. William Bent was the first to recover and he rose in indignation, snapping, "What the hell is the meaning of this, Chevalier? You were warned to stay away from this post."

"So we were, Bill," Pierre said. "And I intended to do as you so unjustly wanted." He took a step closer to Nate. "But then I was watching through my telescope, waiting for this pig to leave the fort so we could finish the business between us, and I saw him talking to Becknell. Now why would he do that? I asked myself. And I wondered if maybe he was planning to hook up with the caravan and travel to Santa Fe." The voyageur scowled. "I couldn't take the chance of that happening. Getting close to him then would be too hard to do what with the men of the caravan ready to shoot at anything that moves."

"So you snuck back in here?" Ceran St. Vrain said. "How dare you!"

"It was quite easy. All we had to do was blend in with

one of the groups from the caravan and your lookout never spotted us.''

Bent jabbed a finger at the front door. "Leave, now, and there will be no hard feelings.''

"I'm afraid I can't,'' Pierre said, focusing on Nate. "This is just between the two of us. My friends will make certain no one interferes.''

Nate, holding a cup of coffee in his right hand, stared down the barrel of Chevalier's rifle and wished he was sitting straighter so he could get at his flintlocks. Keeping his voice level, he asked, "Are you going to kill me without giving me a chance to defend myself?''

"Not at all,'' Pierre answered. "This will be a fair fight, I assure you.''

It was then that Francisco Gaona stood, his hands hanging loosely at his sides. "Pardon me, *señor,* but this man is a friend of mine and I can not stand by and do nothing while you impose your will on us.''

Chevalier looked at the Mexican as if he was inspecting a new animal species for the very first time. Snorting, he said with contempt, "No one asked your opinion, greaser. Sit down and keep your mouth shut until this is over.''

Gaona's features darkened perceptibly. He glanced at the men on either side of Chevalier and an odd smile creased his lips. "I do not like having guns pointed my way. Kindly have your *amigos* lower theirs or suffer the consequences.''

The voyageurs exchanged glances and laughed.

"What can you do?'' Chevalier asked disdainfully.

"This,'' Francisco said, and moved, his hands invisible as he swept both pistols from his sash, cocking them as he drew. The two shots boomed as one. Chevalier's friends were hit, each in the shoulder. Both staggered and dropped their rifles as the balls ripped through them. Both clutched at their wounds, one falling to his knees.

Belatedly, Pierre uttered a bestial growl and pivoted
to aim his gun at Francisco, but as if by magic Francisco
had transferred his right-hand pistol to his left and a
smaller pistol had blossomed in its place, pointed at
Pierre's head. Pierre turned to granite.

"You will be so kind as to drop your rifle, *por favor*,"
Francisco said.

Chevalier hesitated. His thumb, which rested on the
hammer of his rifle, twitched for all to behold. Everyone
knew he was tempted to shoot. All he had to do was
cock that hammer and fire. Then he took a good look at
Gaona's smaller pistol and saw that it was already
cocked. His face crimson with suppressed rage, he lowered his rifle to the floor, then straightened. "Now what,
you bastard?"

"What happens next is up to Señor King," Francisco
responded.

Nate slowly rose, all eyes on him. He set down his
cup and stepped clear of the chair. Since he was the one
Pierre had challenged, what happened next was entirely
up to him. He could ask Bent to have Pierre thrown off
the fort again, but doing so would leave the greater issue
unresolved. And as sure as people loved to gossip, there
would be talk. The trappers and others would learn what
had transpired and they would spread the word to those
they met. Within a few months everyone living in the
Rockies would know that he had refused to stand up to
Chevalier and his courage would come into question. He
dared not let that happen. Of all human virtues, the Indians and the mountain men alike valued and respected
courage the most. If he wanted to be able to hold his head
up at the Rendezvous, he had to answer the challenge in
the only way possible. "How do you want to do this?"
he asked.

The voyageur smirked and reached behind his back.

Out came a large butcher knife, the blade gleaming in the lantern light. "Will this do?"

Nodding, Nate removed his pistols and placed them on the table beside Winona. For an instant her gaze caught his. He could practically feel her soul reaching out to him and his resolve faltered, but only for a second. Pulling his knife, he confronted his adversary. "Ready when you are."

"Now just hold on!" Bent declared. "Since I'm part owner of this post, I have a say in what goes on here. And one of our ironclad rules is that there will be no fighting on the premises."

"We can make no exceptions," St. Vrain added.

"Very well," Pierre said. "First take care of my friends. Then let's take this outside the walls where we'll have all the room in the world. How say you, King?"

Nate nodded.

Soon a mass exodus ensued, with word of the fight spreading like wildfire among all those at the fort and, thanks to swift runners, those at the wagons and even in the Cheyenne village. Scores and scores of people poured through the gates and streamed from the camps and the lodges. They formed into a gigantic crescent with the open end at the front of the fort. Inevitably, bets were placed, with men shouting back and forth as they offered and accepted odds.

Of all this activity Nate was barely conscious. He was thinking of Winona and Zach and what would happen to them should he lose. And lose he might. Pierre Chevalier was not to be taken lightly. No matter how well Nate fought, a single slip or mistake could cost him his life. What would happen to his loved ones then?

Such worry wasn't new to him. A free trapper never knew from one day to the next whether he would be alive to greet the following dawn. Every time he ventured forth on a trapping trip, he couldn't help but speculate on whether he would see his cabin again. The grim nature of life in the often-savage wilderness dictated that every man must stay constantly on his guard or risk forfeiting the life he held so dear. Hostiles, grizzlies, disease, accidents, they all claimed trappers at an appalling rate. Some old-timers claimed that out of every five men who boldly ventured into the Rockies, only one would ever make it out again.

His only consolation was that should he perish, life would go on. Winona and Zach would eventually recover enough to get on with their lives. Winona, unfortunately, would be compelled by necessity to remarry. Single women were at a decided disadvantage in a warrior-dominated society; only the men were permitted to hunt buffalo, the staple of Indian life.

Nate bowed his head, girding himself, banishing his morbid thoughts. Long ago he had learned that if a man wanted to win a fight, he had to *believe* he was going to win it with every atom of his being. Attitude was all-important. As with every aspect of life, a positive outlook invariably meant the difference between success and failure.

A hand fell gently on his shoulder, and he looked up into the kindly face of his mentor. They knew each other so well, they had been through so much together, that words weren't needed. The hardships they had endured had forged their friendship into an unbreakable bond. Still, Nate spoke. "If anything should happen to me, watch over Winona and Zach."

"Do you think I'd do otherwise?"

They were standing just outside the gate. Nate surveyed the crowd and felt self-conscious. He hadn't meant for the dispute to become so public an issue. Off to one side were Bent, St. Vrain, and Becknell in earnest conversation. Chevalier stood waiting a dozen yards away. "Keep your eyes on the crowd," Nate said. "Pierre might have other friends."

"Don't fret. If anyone so much as touches a weapon, he's dead."

Nate steeled his will and strode forward. He heard Zach calling his name, but he refused to look back. Now, more than ever, he mustn't weaken.

Pierre also heard. "Isn't that your brat, King? Don't you care that soon he'll be crying over your grave?"

"Go to hell."

"One day, Grizzly Killer, I undoubtedly will. But today it is your turn. And maybe, afterward, I will stop by to see your wife."

Right then and there Nate would have attacked, but the three traders suddenly joined them.

"We want several things made clear," Bent declared. "None of us approve of this feud. You're setting a bad example for the other trappers, and I wouldn't be surprised if in the future we have to work a lot harder to maintain order."

"You make me want to cry, *mon ami*," Chevalier said in mock sorrow, then roared with laughter.

"I fail to see the humor," Bent stated testily.

"So do I," St. Vrain said, and looked at Nate and the voyageur. "Must you resort to this drastic step? Can't we sit down like gentlemen and discuss the matter? Perhaps we can avoid bloodshed."

"Save your breath, Ceran," Pierre snapped. "This is a matter of personal honor with me. If you had fire in your veins instead of ice, you would better understand."

Nate knew the traders were wasting their time if they hoped to prevail on Chevalier to change his mind. He was going to tell them as much when a lean, gray-haired stranger dressed in homespun clothes walked from among the spectators and came toward them.

"Who is this?" Pierre asked.

"Crain, a trader in dry goods," Becknell revealed. "This is his first trip to Santa Fe."

The lean man smiled and nodded at each of them, then turned to the wagon master. "Bill, what is going on here? I've just been informed that these two men will fight to the death with knives. Surely such a barbaric practice won't be countenanced."

"I'm afraid it will," Becknell replied.

"We can't permit it, I tell you. We're civilized men, not primitives like those Indians over there."

"Get back with the rest, Mr. Crain," Becknell advised. "If you don't care to watch, return to the wagons. There's nothing you can say or do that will alter matters."

"But whoever wins will be guilty of murder! We have a legal right to stop this atrocity before it goes any further," Crain declared. "Gather enough men and we can lock these two up until they've cooled down."

"I'm afraid you're mistaken about our legal authority in this case, Mr. Crain," William Bent interjected. "You see, there is no law here, not in the sense of an organized legal system such as exists back in the States. There isn't a law officer within hundred of miles of this spot."

"But . . ." Crain began.

Bent held up a hand. "Let me finish. You're like a lot of men when they first head out this way. You mistakenly think that the same rule of law applies west of the Mississippi that applies east of it, and you're wrong. Out here a man is his own law."

"That's anarchy!" Crain blurted.

"It's freedom, sir. True freedom. Back in the States a man gives up his right to do as he pleases. In exchange for false security, he lets the government run his life, lets himself be ruled by the dictates of politicians instead of the dictates of his own mind and heart." He paused. "If these men want to settle their dispute with knives, out here they have that right.''

"I've never heard such foolishness," Crain said in disgust, and glanced at Nate and Pierre. "If you two simpletons are so intent on killing yourselves, go ahead." So saying, he stomped off, his back as stiff as a board.

Chevalier grinned. "There are jackasses everywhere, it seems." Sobering, he hefted his knife and faced Nate. "But enough talk, eh, King? Let us, as they say, get down to business."

Then, unexpectedly, Pierre attacked.

Chapter Six

Nate had expected the voyageur to wait until the three traders were out of harm's way before beginning the fight, so he was taken unawares when Chevalier suddenly lunged and stabbed at his chest. Only his pantherish reflexes saved him. He threw himself to the right, sweeping his knife up, and barely managed to deflect the thrust. Their blades rang together. Continuing to move, to circle, he sought an opening.

Bent, St. Vrain, and Becknell were walking rapidly away.

"I almost had you, Grizzly Killer," Pierre said cockily, lowering into a crouch and holding his knife close to his waist. "And we've only just begun."

Refusing to respond, to break his concentration, Nate circled and waited. He did as Shakespeare had taught him, fixing his eyes on Chevalier's knife. When it flicked out, he backed up. When it slashed at his body, he twisted and dodged. When it arced high, he ducked low. And all the while he looked for his chance.

Many of the onlookers were yelling and cheering. To the trappers this was the equivalent of high entertainment, of the sort they frequently witnessed at the Rendezvous and other gatherings when men who had too much to drink took offense at an imagined or real slur. Only, those fights were usually conducted with fists or as simple wrestling matches.

By their very natures, the trappers and mountain men—those old-timers who no longer trapped for a living but made ends meet as best they could whether living by themselves in a remote cabin or among whichever Indian tribe they happened to favor—were a lusty, hardy bunch. They lived hard, loved hard, fought hard, wringing the most life had to offer out of each and every moment. Regret wasn't in their vocabulary.

So Nate took no offense at the playful shouting and goading of the bystanders. He shut out the noise, focusing on Chevalier, his knife extended, edge out, for a quick swipe. But he purposefully didn't swing as often as he could have. He gave the impressions of being timid, of being unwilling to overextend himself and risk injury. There was a reason behind his behavior, which soon became apparent.

Pierre grew increasingly confident the longer the fight went. He grew bolder, darting in closer and closer in his eagerness to bury his blade into Nate. His swings weren't quite as controlled, his movements a bit less precise.

Still Nate held back. Several times he might have scored, but he passed up the opportunities. He craved a decisive win. If he merely nicked his foe, the voyageur would become cautious and be more difficult to defeat.

"What's taking you so long, Chevalier?" someone in the throng called out above all the rest.

Pierre's cheeks reddened and he growled. Taking a step rearward so he was beyond Nate's reach, he snapped, "Did you hear that, King? That's what I get for going easy on you."

"We can still lower our weapons and shake hands," Nate said, breaking his silence.

"Never."

Nate stopped circling. He had to be certain. "Tell me, Chevalier. What happens if I should only wound you? Will you let bygones be bygones? Can we go our separate ways in peace?"

"You will never know peace as long as I'm alive!"

"That's what I was afraid you'd say," Nate said, and feinted. Pierre countered, Nate evaded the knife, and they resumed circling. A lightning strike at Nate's right wrist would have connected if Nate hadn't leaped out of the way.

The voyageur's eagerness was giving way to impatience, and impatience was wedded to recklessness. Pierre attempted to disembowel Nate. Failing, he cursed, shifted, and drove his knife at Nate's neck.

Gliding in and under the blow was child's play. In front of Nate was Chevalier's unprotected abdomen, and with a swift thrust Nate ripped the man's buckskin shirt and the skin underneath, but not severely. Pierre, horrified, pressed a hand to the wound and backed away, shock slowing him down.

Nate took another long stride and saw the voyageur's knife sweep at his neck. Jerking aside, he felt a puff of air as the blade flashed past. Then, pivoting sharply, he whipped his knife upward and plunged it into Pierre's knife hand.

Chevalier howled. His weapon fell as he wrenched his hand loose, causing blood to spray all over him and the ground. Agony etching his features, he tried to flee.

But Nate wasn't going to let him. He pounced, raining

the knife down on Pierre's face, using the hilt not the blade to batter the voyageur's cheeks and lips. Chevalier staggered, then raised his arms to ward off more blows.

Nate was relentless. He slammed his left fist into Pierre's stomach, and followed through with a left to Pierre's chin. Down the man went, crashing onto his back, stunned yet not out. Pierre rose on an elbow and grabbed at Nate's legs with his good hand, which was a mistake because in so doing he exposed that hand to Nate's knife, and paid for his oversight when the bloody blade pierced his palm.

Arching his spine, Chevalier wailed like a wounded wolf. "No more! No more!"

Heedless of the appeal, Nate tore his knife free and stood over his enemy. He gripped the front of Pierre's shirt and elevated the butcher knife overhead for a death stroke. Pierre froze, eyes wide in terror. The crowd fell deathly still. All Nate heard was a roaring in his ears, the roaring of his blood as it raced through his veins. He had Chevalier right where he wanted him. All it would take was a single stroke and the voyageur would never bother anyone else ever again. His arm was poised and tensed for the kill.

Suddenly a single voice broke the silence, the plaintive call of a young boy in turmoil. "Don't, Pa!"

Tense seconds passed. Slowly Nate's muscles relaxed and his arm dropped. He shoved Pierre flat on the ground, then straightened. "You can thank your lucky stars, fool, that I'm raising him to believe there's a God in Heaven."

"What?" Pierre blurted out weakly, not comprehending. "What's that you say?"

Nate felt an odd weariness flood through him, and with it a feeling of immense satisfaction. Turning away, he saw his wife and son and stepped toward them. The great cheer that burst from scores of lips stopped him, and the next moment he was inundated by people pressing in from all sides to congratulate him and clap him on the back. He nodded numbly and let them buffet him this way and that, until abruptly a white-haired raging bull, pushing through to his side, scattered those in front with a warning.

"Let him pass, damn your hides, or there will be hell to pay!"

They parted, made meek by Shakespeare's wrath, and offered no interference as the mountain man escorted Nate over to Winona and Zach.

William Bent appeared out of nowhere. "You did fine, King. Real fine. No one will hold this against you, and once the word gets out, even Chevalier's friends will leave you alone."

"Let's hope so," Nate said, about to drape his arm around Winona's shoulders when he saw that he still held his knife, the blade dripping blood. Crouching, he wiped it clean on the grass, then stuck it in his sheath.

Francisco Gaona came over, his hand outstretched. "I would like to offer my congratulations also, *señor*. I have seen many knife fighters in my time and you are one of the best."

"I could say the same about you with pistols," Nate replied, shaking hands, impressed by Francisco's sincerity. He found himself liking the Mexican more and more as time went on.

"Much practice, *señor*," Francisco said. "My *padre* gave me my first *pistola* when I was but ten years old."

Small fingers touched Nate's own, and he looked down into the anxious upturned face of his son. He smiled reassuringly and gave Zach's fingers a tender squeeze. "Everything is all right now."

"I was scared again, Pa," the boy said softly. "Only this time I was scared for you."

"That makes two of us."

Shakespeare cleared his throat, rubbed a hand in

Zach's hair, and announced, "What say we cut short this palaver and go in for some drinks. I'm buying."

"Will wonders nerve cease," Nate declared.

They weren't the only ones desirous of quenching their thirsts. The room was packed. Many of the patrons saw fit to recount the fight over and over, with those who had won money extolling Nate's skill while those who had lost debated the mistakes Chevalier had made and related how they would have fought differently to insure they won.

Bent and St. Vrain secured a corner table. Nate let McNair buy him a whiskey, although he would rather have gone with Winona, Blue Water Woman, and Zach to their guest rooms. He took a tentative sip, and winced as the burning liquid scorched a path down his throat.

"Strong stuff," Shakespeare said, grinning. "Bent here doesn't believe in watering his drinks down like some shady tavern owners I've known do." He winked at Nate. "Of course, I can't say if he does the same for the Indians."

"I'd never cheat a customer," the trader said indignantly. "Everyone knows that, which is why even the Kiowas trade with me. They know they'll get a fair deal." He tipped his drink. "Honesty is always the best policy."

"An admirable trait, to be sure," Francisco commented, and gazed at Nate and McNair. "So perhaps it is only fitting that I be honest with the two of you."

"How so?" Shakespeare asked.

"If I may be so bold, *señor,* I would like to ask why you are going to Santa Fe?"

"Because it's a hell of a lot closer than Paris," Shakespeare joked. "Actually, because we're in need of a frolic and Santa Fe is as friendly a city as you'll find anywhere."

"Not anymore," Francisco said soberly.

"I'm afraid he's right," Becknell chimed in. "Santa Fe isn't like it was back when you were there last. The attitude of the authorities has changed, and so has that of many of the people."

"Some of the people," Francisco amended.

"Care to enlighten us?" Shakespeare said.

William Becknell sighed. "It all started several years ago. I began to notice that a few of the people I deal with weren't as hospitable as they used to be. One or two avoided me. Then pretty soon it spread. I was puzzled at first, until I realized that they had been seeing us at our worst for years and that sooner or later this was bound to happen."

McNair nodded thoughtfully. "I understand."

"Well I don't," Nate said, wondering about the implications for their visit and the treatment his family would receive.

"It's like this," Becknell elaborated. "Since I first opened up the Santa Fe Trail, caravan after caravan has paid Santa Fe a visit with just one purpose in the minds of the traders who go there. Namely, to get rich quick, to reap enormous profits they couldn't possibly earn anywhere else." He paused. "It's greed, pure and simple, and greed never fails to bring out all that's ugly in us."

"When the traders and wagoners get there," Shakespeare said, taking up the explanation when Becknell stopped, "they tend to cut loose a mite more than they should. They drink, they gamble, they spend their nights with the painted ladies. In short, they just raise sheer hell."

"Who can blame them?" This from Bent. "After traveling over eight hundred miles through hostile Indian country, and having to contend with a burning desert part of the way, no wonder they're ready for some fun and relaxation."

"But now some of the citizens of Santa Fe have grown tired of the rowdy behavior," Becknell continued. "They regard us Americans as more of a nuisance than a blessing."

"Then why don't they just come out and say that they don't want any more caravans to pay them a visit?" Nate asked.

"It's not as simple as that," Becknell answered. "They need the goods we bring. They can't get them anywhere else. So they tolerate our coming, but the authorities have put a stop to the wild celebrating. And a lot of the common people avoid us when we show up. They won't have anything to do with us."

Francisco Gaona, who had been attentively listening in uncomfortable silence, now spoke. "Not all the common people, *señor*. Many of us realize we owe a great debt to you Americans. Before your caravans started coming, we had to travel many hundreds of miles to the south through the heart of Apache country to buy those things you now bring to us, and often we had to pay more than we pay you." He folded his hands on the table. "No, you have done us a great service. I think part of the problem is that my own government has become too greedy and they resent that the traders are unwilling to pay more."

"What do you mean?" Nate inquired.

It was Becknell who answered. "The authorities in New Mexico have the power to charge us whatever customs duties they want to impose, most of which goes into their own pockets. To keep the duties reasonably low, we have to pay bribes. Lots of bribes. Everyone from the governor all the way down to the customhouse clerks wants their share." He scowled. "Most of us resent having to give up a portion of our hard-earned profits for the benefit of crooked petty officials and his obesity, the governor."

"How does all of this apply to us?" Nate asked. "We're not going to Santa Fe to trade."

"The bad feelings are so general that some of the mountain men who have gone to Santa Fe for a good time have found themselves tossed into jail if they step the least bit out of line. A few have been set upon by local rowdies," Becknell replied.

"Please don't think badly of my people," Francisco said quickly. "We are not all like that."

Nate, disturbed by the news, took a swallow. Dare he take his family into the middle of such a powder keg? What was to stop the New Mexican authorities from throwing him in jail if he inadvertently did something wrong?

Shakespeare didn't share his misgivings. "Thanks for the warnings," the mountain man told Becknell and Francisco, "but this doesn't change our minds none. If we're on our best behavior we won't be bothered. And I really would like to see Santa Fe again. I have a few friends living there who I haven't seen in a coon's age."

"And you, *señor*?" Francisco asked Nate.

"I'll talk it over with my wife, but I'd imagine she'll want to keep on going if Blue Water Woman and this old buzzard aren't turning back."

"Excellent. Then perhaps you will do me the honor of staying at my *hacienda* during your visit? It is only fifteen miles outside of the city."

"We wouldn't want to impose," Nate said.

"Nonsense. Having you and your family as guests would be a treat for my own family. It would not be an imposition at all." Francisco looked at McNair. "My invitation holds true for you also, *señor*."

"Then I reckon we'll take you up on it. Maybe you can help me track down some of my old friends. One of them is named . . ." Shakespeare suddenly stopped to stare intently at the entrance.

A general hush fell over the room, silencing every man there. Nate looked around, and was shocked to see Pierre Chevalier framed in the doorway. The voyageur wasn't wearing a shirt. Both his hands and his abdomen had been heavily bandaged. His black and blue face was badly swollen. His lips were puffy. He spied Nate and advanced, saying nothing to those who voiced a word of greeting.

"Not again," Shakespeare muttered.

Chevalier halted a yard from Nate and gave a curt nod. "I'll keep this short, American. I know enough to admit when I've made a mistake, and I'm man enough to own up to it. I challenged you and you beat me, fair and square. So as far as I'm concerned, the matter is settled."

Nate was too flabbergasted to say a word.

"How about you?" Chevalier asked. "If you insist on satisfying your honor, I'll meet you wherever and whenever you want once my hands have healed."

"My honor is satisfied," Nate said, finding his voice.

"Good. Then there will be no hard feelings between us." Chevalier nodded, smiled, and departed.

"Well, I'll be damned!" Shakespeare exclaimed after the voyageur was gone and murmuring broke out all around them. "He's more of a man than I figured."

"Can you trust him?" Francisco asked.

"I hope so," Nate said.

"Whether you can or whether you can't, by this time tomorrow it won't matter," Becknell mentioned. "We'll be well on our way to Santa Fe by then."

"I'll drink to that," Nate said, and did so.

To their right rose green foothills that served as mere footstools for the towering Rockies beyond. To their left stretched the well-nigh limitless prairie, a sea of grass teeming with buffalo, antelope, and deer.

Nate admired the scenery on both sides as he rode

southward at the head of the four long lines of wagons. In front of him were William Becknell and Francisco Gaona. His family was on one side, Shakespeare and Blue Water Woman on the other. Across his thighs rested his Hawken.

Long ago they had lost sight of Bent's Fort. Bent and St. Vrain had come out to wish them well and make them promise to stop by on their return trip; then the pair had stood and waved every so often as the lumbering wagons rolled off. Eventually the fort had become a black dot in the distance, and ultimately had vanished in the haze.

The burning sun made men and animals alike lethargic. The wagoners had to crack their whips repeatedly to keep their mules and oxen going. At the rear of the columns rose a cloud of choking dust, which explained why Nate had graciously accepted Becknell's invitation to ride up front with him.

"Say Pa," Zach said. "I've been meaning to ask you why they have the wagons strung out in four rows instead of one?"

Becknell overheard and turned in the saddle. "It's a precaution, son, in case we have to move fast should hostiles attack. At the first sign of them, I give the order and the muleteers form the wagons into a big square."

"Gosh. Do you think we'll be attacked?" Zach asked.

"I doubt it," Becknell said. "Even the Comanches will think twice about raiding a wagon train this size."

"What about the Apaches?"

"They're a different story entirely. I've had those devils slip right into our camp and slit the throat of some poor unfortunate while he slept."

"You have?" Zach said, aghast.

The trader promptly realized his mistake and hastened to add, "But that hasn't happened in three or four years, as I recollect. Most Apache activity is now concentrated

south and southwest of Santa Fe, not in the mountains to
the north.''

''Do you post guards at night?''

''Lots of guards.''

''If you need help, let us know. Samson and I want to
do our share of the work.''

''I'll keep you in mind,'' Becknell promised.

The Father of the Santa Fe Trail, from long experience,
knew exactly where the best spots to make night camp
were situated, spots where there was plenty of water for
everyone and sufficient forage for the stock. This first
night they halted at the base of a high foothill. After the
square was formed, the mules, oxen, and horses were let
loose to graze and cook fires were started.

Winona and Blue Water Woman were the only women
in the entire company, and the muleteers went out of
their way to treat them both with the utmost courtesy.
Where normally the wagoners used five swear words in
a six-word sentence, they now conducted themselves like
perfect gentlemen in the presence of the ladies. As the
pair strolled around the encampment they were treated to
polite bows or the touching of hats in the most exaggerated civil manner.

Nate came on Shakespeare squatting by a fire and
heard his friend's throaty chuckles. ''What has you
amused?'' he wanted to know.

''I'm thinking of how happy these muleteers will be
to reach Santa Fe. I expect that city is going to be in for
a fit of cussing like none other in human history.''

''Why do you say that?''

''Because these muleteers can no more curb their
tongues for long than a grizzly can curb its appetite.
They'll have a lot of catching up to do when they get
there.''

Twilight enveloped the land when the evening meal

was completed. Becknell, Francisco Gaona, and several wagoners came over to socialize. They were all listening, enthralled, to Shakespeare tell about the time he was captured by the Blackfeet, when a skinny muleteer bearing a rifle approached.

Becknell saw the man and stood. "What are you doing here, Mullins?" he demanded. "You're supposed to be on guard duty."

"That I am, sir. But I figured this was more important."

"What is?"

"The fact we have company calling, sir."

"Company?" Becknell said. "Damn it all, man. For once can't you get right to the point? Who would come visiting us out in the middle of nowhere?"

"Why," Mullins said, "who else, sir, but a pack of murdering Comanches?"

Chapter Seven

There were only four of them, four young warriors whose proud and fearless bearing was in stark contrast to the nervous fidgeting of the two dozen muleteers and traders who held rifles fixed on the quartet. Their bronzed faces were painted for war, and they were variously armed with lances, bows, knives, and one inferior old flintlock of the type often traded to the northern tribes by the Hudson's Bay Company.

Nate stayed close to Becknell as the wagon master pushed through the line of whites. He saw the tallest of the Comanches scrutinize him, then gaze past him to stare at Shakespeare.

Without preliminaries the tall warrior's hands moved in sign language. "This is Comanche territory. You are not wanted here."

Becknell went to lift his hands, then hesitated. "Where's Shultz?" he asked a nearby muleteer. "He speaks sign better than I do."

"Allow me," Nate volunteered, stepping forward. He translated the Comanche's words.

"What's this devil up to?" Becknell mused aloud. "He knows that we know this is Comanche land and that we're going through whether they like the notion or not."

"Let's find out," Nate said, facing the tall warrior. "What is it our Comanche brothers wish? Why do they honor us with this visit?" he signed.

Surprise flickered across the warrior's features. "No white man has ever called a Comanche his brother before," he responded, his hands flowing gracefully as he formed the signs. "Who are you?"

"I am called Grizzly Killer."

"How is it that you have an Indian name?"

"My people are the Shoshones."

The Comanche's dark, fathomless eyes raked Nate from head to toe. "You do not look like any Shoshone I have ever seen."

Smiling, Nate answered, "They are my adopted people. My wife is Shoshone. My son is being raised to honor the Shoshone ways."

"You are one of those who lives in the high mountains and catches beaver for their hides?"

"Yes."

"I have heard of such men."

A strained silence ensued as the tall warrior surveyed the wagons and the stock within the square. At length he signed, "I fought Shoshones once. They fought bravely, as men should fight. They have my respect and you have my respect." He made a gesture of contempt at the line of traders and muleteers. "These others are less than dogs, but they may go their way in peace." He uttered a piercing yip, and all four of them wheeled their war ponies and dashed off across the prairie into the gathering darkness.

"What was that all about?" Becknell asked, perplexed.

Shakespeare stepped closer. "It's my guess they're part of a large band and they were fixing to raid us later tonight. Those four came in to look us over, to count our guns and horses and see where we might be vulnerable. But now they've changed their minds. If not for Nate, some of us would be pushing up buffalo grass come morning."

"What did he do? I didn't catch all of that between them?"

Nate walked away as McNair explained. He found Winona, Zach, and Blue Water Woman waiting anxiously to hear what had happened, so he simply informed them that the Comanches weren't going to cause any trouble.

"That's good to hear, Pa," his son said. "But it's the Apaches I'm worried about. I hope they don't give us any trouble either."

"You're getting yourself worked up for no reason," Nate assured him. "I'd never let the Apaches get you. You know that. You're as safe as if you were back home in our cabin."

Winona gave him a long, hard look, but she said nothing.

The next couple of weeks tended to bear Nate out. Their days passed uneventfully, and their nights were undisturbed. Because Becknell was taking the Mountain Route and not the Cimarron Cutoff there was ample water all along the way. Twice they did see Indian smoke signals in the distance, but the Indians left them alone.

When, at last, the wagon train negotiated the Sangre de Cristo Mountains and crested a last low rise, before the overjoyed wagoners unfolded the sprawling whitewashed city they had traveled so far to reach. At the sight of their destination the traders and muleteers whooped in delight, fired their guns, and waved their hats.

Nate was equally thrilled on seeing the many flat-topped roofs crowning the neatly arranged adobe-brick buildings. He squinted in the bright sunlight at patches of green on many of the roofs and said aloud, "I'll be darned if that doesn't look like grass."

"It is, *señor*."

Turning, Nate found Francisco Gaona riding beside him. "I've never heard of grass roofs before."

"The roofs themselves are made of heavy timbers," Francisco revealed. "On top is piled a thick layer of earth, then grass seed is spread around and let to grow."

"Amazing."

"There is a method to our apparent madness, *señor*. You will find that it gets very hot here, hotter by far than anywhere you have ever been, and the earth helps keep the rooms cool during the heat of the day. For this same reason the walls of our buildings are much thicker than those in your country."

The rutted track they had been following merged into a road bearing westward into Santa Fe. At the side of the road, watching the wagons go by, stood an old man dressed in a plain white cotton shirts and pants. A straw sombrero protected his head from the sun. He was holding a rope lead in his left hand, and strung out behind him were six burros laden with large bundles of chopped mountain scrub pine.

"Firewood?" Nate asked.

"*Sí*," Francisco answered. "Yes, it is firewood. *Piñon*, we call it. At this time of year the days are hot but the nights are cold. That old man will sell all he has gathered in the city."

Further on they encountered two riders heading into the mountains. Both were well dressed in expensive clothes and sombreros. In addition, gaily colored blankets with slits in the center for their heads had been draped over their shoulders.

At a question from Nate, Francisco said, "Those are called *ponchos,* my friend. And those men are *caballeros.* 'Gentlemen,' I believe you would say in English."

The *caballeros* called out greetings to Gaona as they went by, and he returned the favor.

Soon they were close enough to see people moving about along the streets. Nate marveled that there were so many, until he remembered the city boasted a population of three thousand. When all the surrounding ranches and other estates were taken into account, there were close to four thousand local inhabitants.

Zach rode up on Nate's right side. "Isn't this wonderful, Pa?"

"It's an education," Nate said.

The road entered Santa Fe from the east. Many of the pedestrians stopped to stare, while the rest just went about their business. Nate and his companions started to cross a wide street, and as Nate glanced to his right he spied a huge church silhouetted against the background of the snowcapped Sangre de Cristo range.

"That is our cathedral," Francisco said, sitting straighter in the saddle. "If you like, we will go there during your stay."

The innocent proposal gave Nate pause. For some reason it made him feel oddly uncomfortable. Maybe, he told himself, it was because he hadn't attended church in years, not since that day long ago when he left New York City for the unknown lands beyond the frontier. Zach, he realized with a start, had never set foot in a house of worship. Doing so might do the boy some good. "We'd be pleased to go," he said.

Suddenly an immense plaza opened up ahead, and Becknell led the wagons toward the customhouse situated at the north side of the public square. Along the south side was a row of shops. On the east side farmers had spread out blankets on the ground and were busily peddling vegetables, melons, bread, and more. A long, low building on the west side of the plaza was distinguished by a tall flagpole in front, from which hung the Mexican flag.

"That is the governor's palace," Francisco mentioned when he saw where Nate was looking. Then he added rather ominously, "It is also the prison."

The square bustled with activity. Nate saw chicken vendors carrying their birds in large wooden cages. There were oxen pulling carts containing sacks of grain. Horsemen rode at their leisure. Dark-haired women sashayed about in the shade. At each corner of the square sat a large cannon. And, to his delight, Nate spotted a man-sized sundial positioned at the very middle of the plaza.

Winona and Blue Water Woman were gazing at everything in awe. This was something no other Shoshone or Flathead woman had ever experienced, and they would have much to tell their relatives and friends when they next visited their respective villages.

Zach stared at one new sight after another, giggling in childish glee.

"If you have no objections, *señor*," Francisco said, "I would like to go to my *hacienda* to see how my family is doing. Tomorrow or the next day, after we are well rested, we will come back to Santa Fe."

Since Nate had already arranged with William Becknell to meet the trader in one week in front of the customhouse to begin their trip back, he was free to do as he pleased. He put Gaona's proposal to his family and friends and they all agreed.

It was late afternoon when the sprawling estate with its tilled fields and large herds of cattle and horses being tended by skilled *vaqueros* came into view. Francisco had spent the ride telling them about early Spanish settlements in the region, and how the Mexicans had carried on after winning their independence in 1821.

Nate was picking up more and more Spanish words as they went along, but he couldn't begin to compete with Winona, who only had to hear a word spoken once and be told its meaning to always use it correctly from that time on. Zach also learned readily. Shakespeare, it turned out, was already fairly well versed in the language. Blue Water Woman, much to Nate's satisfaction, had to work as hard as he did.

Francisco was given a tremendous welcome. *Vaqueros,* servants, and family members streamed from all directions. A beautiful woman in a fashionable blue dress swept into his arms and tearfully kissed him. A young girl of ten joined them, and for a minute no one else disturbed these three as they tenderly embraced.

Then Francisco cleared his throat and introduced his newfound friends to his family. "This is my beloved wife Maria and my daughter Juanita."

The weary travelers were escorted inside while their horses were tended to by servants. Nate gratefully accepted a glass of fruit juice. As he slowly sipped they were given a grand tour, and he was greatly impressed by the many immaculate rooms with their simple but expensive furnishings.

After being afforded the means to wash off the dust of the trail, they were seated at a long table and treated to a sumptuous feast fit for a king. There was wine, beer, *tequila,* juice, milk, and a cinnamon-flavored hot chocolate. There was beef and wheat bread and pastries. And there was traditional Mexican fare: *enchiladas, tostadas, tacos, tamales, frijoles,* and more.

Nate's stomach was ready to burst when he pushed his plate away and leaned back in his chair. "Francisco, if

I ate like this every day I'd be too heavy to climb on my horse.''

"We are strong believers in hospitality, my friend. While you are under my roof all that I have is yours.''

Suddenly a servant appeared. Hurrying up to Francisco, he spoke urgently in Spanish.

"It seems my men have a problem, *señor*,'' Francisco addressed Nate. "Your gelding would not let them remove your saddle at first, and now he will not let them put him in our corral. Perhaps you would be so kind?''

"Gladly,'' Nate said, rising. He stayed on Gaona's heels as they went out the front entrance and around the side to where nine *vaqueros*, who had formed a large circle to prevent Pegasus from getting away, were laughing at the futile efforts of a tenth to get a rope around the gelding's neck. The *vaquero* was trying his best, swinging his *reata* with measured precision, but every trick he tried was foiled by the wily Palouse.

Pegasus would stand still and warily eye the roper until the instant the *reata* flashed out. Then the gelding would dash a few yards and watch as the *vaquero* coiled his rope for another try. Whether the *vaquero* hid the *reata* behind his legs or tried an overhand throw made no difference. Pegasus was always one step ahead of him, moving around the circle of *vaqueros*.

Francisco smiled. "Ignacio will be the brunt of many jokes in the weeks ahead. He is the best roper on the *hacienda* and until now there hasn't been a horse he couldn't catch. Perhaps you should spare him from further humiliation.''

Nate stepped forward, between a pair of *vaqueros*, and straight over to Pegasus. The ranch hands all fell silent, observing with interest as the gelding snorted, then rubbed its head against him like an oversized puppy. He stroked Pegasus's neck and whispered in its ears.

Ignacio, a lean man with a wide black *sombrero*, a

brown jacket, and brown pants that flared out at the bottom, walked up and sadly shook his head. He glanced around as Francisco approached, and said something in Spanish.

"He would like to know where you obtained such a magnificent animal," Gaona translated. "None of my men have ever seen a horse such as this."

Nate briefly detailed how he received the gelding as a gift from the Nez Percé.

"It is unfortunate they saw fit to castrate him," Francisco lamented, "or I would be tempted to buy him from you so he can sire a line that would make my *rancho* the talk of New Mexico."

"I would never sell him," Nate said. "He means as much to me as my son's dog means to him."

"Then you are an *hombre* after my own heart," Francisco said. "I too love horses." He pointed at the corral. "Which is why I had this built a few years ago so we can keep watch over our best stock at night. The Apaches used to come in this close to Santa Fe quite regularly, but they no longer do. Still, I play it safe, as you say in your country. I have insisted that three or four *vaqueros* always go with my wife and daughter when they go for their daily ride."

Nate took Pegasus to the corral, then paused to admire the broad vista of beautiful countryside visible in all directions. The ranch was located in a lush valley watered by a swift running stream. From the abundance of green grass and trees the soil was ideal for tilling. To the southeast rose hills. Far to the south and west were more high mountains. "This land is almost as pretty as the northern Rockies," he commented.

"Almost?" Francisco said, and laughed. "There is no more lovely land anywhere as far as I am concerned. For four generations my family has lived here, has fought here, has died here. And through it all we have prospered.

When my time comes, I want to be buried on that hill to the west where my father and his father and his father before him are all buried, and on that day the son I hope to have before too long will take over this land and continue the good fight.'' His eyes sparkled as he spoke and his face shown with profound inner pride.

''I hope all that you wish comes true, friend,'' Nate said.

Just then the *vaquero* named Ignacio rejoined them and spoke to Gaona. Several minutes were spent in earnest conversation, and when Francisco turned to Nate there were worry lines around his eyes.

''This is not good.''

''What?'' Nate inquired.

''I have just been informed that during my absence the Apaches raided an estate twenty-five miles northwest of here and another fifteen miles to the southeast. Close to thirty people were killed, including women and children.''

''Do you expect trouble here?''

''Not really. My estate is one of the largest in the territory. I have forty-one *vaqueros* and they are all brave men. The Apaches know they would pay dearly for an attack.'' Francisco gazed at the distant mountains. ''The estates that were raided are much smaller than mine. We have nothing to fear.''

Nate couldn't help but notice that Gaona's tone belied his statement. He debated whether to stay at the *hacienda* or to return to the security of Santa Fe. There were plenty of hotels where they could stay. But he disliked doing so since it might hurt Francisco's feelings. As if Gaona could read minds, he unexpectedly spoke.

''I would not like for anything to happen while you and your family are my guests, *señor*. During your stay I will make certain all my men stay close at hand and I will have guards posted each night. You need not worry about your loved ones.''

"Thank you," Nate said, his mind made up. It was highly unlikely the Apaches would dare go up against such a large force of competent fighting men. He would stay.

"There is still some daylight left. Would you care to go for a short ride? I'll show you some of this land I hold so dear."

"I'd be delighted," Nate said.

Vaqueros saddled fresh horses, and they were soon making a circuit of the thriving ranch, attended by six armed men. As they rode off Nate glanced back at the house, wondering what had happened to Shakespeare. The mountain man, he decided, must be entertaining the ladies with tall tales of his exploits, or else regaling Mrs. Gaona with quotes from old William S. He did see Zach and Juanita by a tree, talking and laughing and thoroughly enjoying one another.

The Gaona family had developed the land wisely over the years. They had dug irrigation ditches from the stream to water the tilled acreage, which was just enough to meet the food needs of the estate with a little extra produced to trade for needed goods. The rest of the land was maintained in its pristine state and afforded abundant grazing for a huge herd of cattle. There were also many fine horses and dozens of mules. Each year some of the best mules were culled and sold in Santa Fe for tidy sums since there was such a huge demand for the animals.

Wildlife was present in great numbers. Nate saw dozens of chipmunks and several colonies of prairie dogs. Rabbits often bounded off in alarm at their approach. He also saw coyote sign—and once, at the stream, the tracks of a bobcat, which he pointed out to Francisco.

"Are you a skilled tracker, *señor*?"

"Some might say so," Nate said, "but I don't hold a candle to McNair. That man can follow a fly across a desert."

"Really?" Francisco grinned. "I have a few good trackers in my employ, although I am afraid they have not yet learned how to track something through thin air."

"I'm sure Shakespeare would be willing to teach them," Nate quipped, and they both laughed.

A rosy twilight sheathed the verdant land when they made their way back to the corral and dismounted. Francisco gave orders to his *vaqueros*, then led the way inside, where they found the mistress of the house laughing over something Shakespeare had told them.

"What outrageous stories are you telling now?" Nate asked, seeking to bait his friend.

"I was just practicing my Spanish by informing Maria about the time you were being chased by a grizzly and you managed to ride smack into a tree limb and get knocked from the saddle."

"Oh."

"And how you thought you were going to die because you were sure your chest was caved in, but all you had was a tiny scratch," Shakespeare went on, eliciting smiles from the women.

"I wish you'd limit your yarns to ones about yourself."

"I would, but they're not half as comical."

"Where's Zach?" Nate asked to change the subject.

Winona rose. "He was playing out back with Juanita the last time I checked on him," she disclosed. "They have become very good friends in such a short time."

"Young'uns have that knack," Shakespeare said. "They're more open with each other than old coons like us. Since they don't put on airs, they have fewer walls to break down."

Taking Winona's hand, Nate walked down a long,

cool hallway to the sturdy back door. Outside was a carefully cultivated flower garden and several cottonwoods. Zach and Juanita were playing tag, chasing each other back and forth among the trees.

"Do you ever wish you were young again?" Nate asked softly, raising Winona's hand to his lips.

"Never," Winona said, leaning against him. "I have never been more content in my life than I am as your wife. You have brought me all the happiness I have ever wanted."

"Even though any of the bravest warriors in your tribe would have leaped at the chance to be your husband? Why, if you'd wanted, you could have married a chief. You'd now be living in the finest of lodges and own more horses than any other Shoshone woman."

Winona's teeth were white in the encroaching darkness. "Treasures of the heart, husband, matter more than treasures we can own."

"Is that a quote from William S.?"

She laughed lightly. "No. It is something I learned from my mother. She taught me that true love matters more than all the horses and lodges in the world. A woman who marries to gain such things goes through life as empty as one of those shells my people sometimes get in trade from the tribes who live close to the big water far to the west. She is lovely on the outside but inside there is nothing."

Looking both ways to be sure no one other than the children happened to be in sight, Nate drew Winona into the shadows, tenderly embraced her, and gave her a lingering, passionate kiss.

"What was that for?" she asked when he broke away.

"My love overflows my heart," Nate said, using the English equivalent of a Shoshone endearment. "You make me proud to be your husband, and I only pray I prove worthy of your trust."

"You already have."

Reluctantly, Nate stepped into the open and called out, "Zach, it's time to come in for the night."

His son stopped running and frowned. "Do we have to, Pa?"

"Yep. Let's go."

"But Juanita and I are having so much fun! She's been teaching me her language and we've been playing games."

"You can learn more and play more tomorrow."

"Awwww. I never get to do what I want."

Nate held the door for them, and gave Winona a peck on the cheek as she followed the youngsters inside. He was about to enter himself when from out of the night to the south came the faint cry of a bird, a warbling call he had never heard before. Pausing, he heard the cry answered from off to the southeast. New Mexico, he reasoned, must have night birds unknown in the northern Rockies. He made a mental note to ask Francisco about them sometime, then closed the door and caught up with his family.

Chapter Eight

Nate's eyes snapped wide open, and he lay in the inky darkness on his back listening to Winona's soft breathing at his side. What had awakened him? he asked himself. By his estimation it must be the middle of the night and everyone in the *hacienda* should be sound asleep. He listened intently but heard nothing. Slowly he started to drift off again, until a low growl sounded in the next room, the room containing Zach and Samson.

Easing quietly upward so as not to disturb Winona, Nate glanced at the closed door separating the two rooms. The mongrel never growled without a reason. Perhaps, he speculated, someone had risen to heed nature's call and Samson had heard them moving about.

The growl was repeated, louder this time.

Annoyed, Nate slipped off the soft bed and padded to the door. He opened it, and was able to distinguish Zach sound asleep on the bed and Samson standing over by the closed door to the corridor. Of half a mind to tie the mongrel outside, Nate walked toward him, then halted in surprise on hearing the same birdcall he'd heard earlier. Only now the call was much louder, seemingly coming from right outside the house. And as before, the cry was answered by another, this time on the opposite side of the house.

A cold chill of premonition swept through Nate and he tensed, scarcely inhaling as he strained to hear more. What a dunderhead he was! Why hadn't he recognized the birdscalls for what they truly were before? Spinning, he hurried back and shook Winona to wake her, first placing his hand over her mouth to prevent an inadvertent outcry.

She woke up instantly, holding herself perfectly still.

"Apaches," Nate whispered. "Get your rifle and stay with Zach. I have to rouse the others."

Winona nodded and stood.

He already had on his leggings. Leaving his shirt and moccasins draped over a chair, he grabbed the Hawken, tucked both flintlocks under his belt, and tiptoed to the hall door. The latch gave without a sound. He peered into the murky corridor but saw no one. Unnerving total quiet reigned in the huge *hacienda*.

Moving in a crouch, he hugged the wall until he reached Shakespeare's room. Soundlessly he worked the latch and glided inside, stopping short on seeing McNair already up and holding a pistol. "I think we have some unwanted visitors," Nate said softly.

"I know. I was coming to fetch you."

"Watch over our wives and Zach. I'll warn Francisco."

"Be careful, son. Apaches are like ghosts when they're on the prowl."

Gaona's bedroom was at the west end of the hallway. Nate stayed low, his back to the wall, his thumb on the rifle's hammer, until he came to the door. Should he knock, he wondered, and risk being heard by the Apaches, or should he go right in? Recalling how handy Francisco was with those fancy polished pistols, Nate decided to lightly rap his knuckles on the smooth wood. He hoped Francisco would come to investigate and not give a shout demanding to know who was there.

There was no response.

Nate glanced at the spacious room fronting the corridor. He made out the outlines of several chairs and over in the corner stood a large bookcase, but nothing else. For a moment doubt assailed him. What if Shakespeare and he were wrong? What if there truly were night birds in the trees outside? He'd feel like an idiot if he was making all this fuss for no reason.

At that very moment one of the chairs abruptly moved.

Nate blinked, thinking his eyes were playing tricks on him, but the chair moved again, creeping a bit nearer to the hallway. His eyes threatened to bulge from their sockets as he probed the gloom to discern details. With a start he saw that the chair wasn't a chair after all but instead was a man hunched low to the floor. And not just any man. It was a stocky Indian naked except for a breechcloth. Even as the realization dawned on him, the figure surged erect and charged, venting a bloodcurdling shriek.

In pure reflex Nate leveled the Hawken, cocked the hammer, and fired from the hip, the gun recoiling in his hands. The onrushing warrior twisted as the ball ripped through him, but kept on coming, raising a knife on high. Nate hurled himself to the right, drawing a flintlock as he did, and got off his shot at the very instant the Apache loomed above him. This time the warrior staggered backwards, clutched at his belly, then collapsed.

The shriek had served as a signal for all hell to break

loose. War whoops echoed from all directions. Gunfire erupted outside. Men yelled and cursed in Spanish. Somewhere horses neighed in fright. From the rear of the house, where the servants were quartered, arose terrified screams.

Gaona's door was flung open and there stood Francisco, shirtless and barefoot, with a flintlock in each hand. He took a step, bumped into the slain Apache, then caught sight of Nate on the floor. "Are you all right, *señor*?"

"Yes," Nate answered, and started to rise.

"Good. I must direct my *vaqueros*. Stay here and don't let the savages get to our families."

Before Nate could say a word, Francisco dashed off. He saw Maria appear in the doorway holding a wrap tight around her body, her face unnaturally pale. "You're better off inside, ma'am," Nate advised, and then recalled she spoke little English. Motioning for her to go back into the room, he closed the door once she complied and turned, scanning the full length of the hall. How could he protect anyone when he only had one loaded gun left? He had to get his ammo pouch and powder horn.

The gunshots, shouts, and whoops outside had reached a crescendo; it sounded as if a war was being waged. But as yet no other Apaches had appeared at either end of the corridor.

Sticking the spent pistol under his belt, Nate drew the other one and ran toward his room. Shakespeare suddenly stepped out in front of him and they nearly collided. "Stand guard," Nate cried. "I'll be right back."

In four bounds he was at Zach's door. Winona, Zach, and Samson were clustered in a corner, Samson with his hair bristling and Winona with her rifle pressed to her shoulder, ready to fire. "Stay close to me," he ordered, not even slowing as he darted into the next bedroom and grabbed his powder horn and bullet pouch. He also scooped up his butcher knife and jammed it, sheath and all, under his belt. Then, running to the hall, he moved swiftly toward Maria Gaona's bedroom.

Blue Water Woman had joined Shakespeare and they were standing back to back, covering both ends of the corridor.

"We should get our families all together in one place," Nate said to McNair. "It'll be easier for them to defend themselves." He indicated Gaona's room. "We'll put them in there."

"Sounds good," Shakespeare replied.

From the rear of the house came a terrifying series of wails and shrieks mixed in with the rapid booming of guns, the din louder and nearer than anything Nate had heard thus far. He feared a large number of Apaches had gained entry and were wreaking havoc among the servants. Constantly glancing at the east end of the hall, he came to Gaona's room just as Maria, holding Juanita close, opened the door. She immediately addressed Shakespeare in Spanish and he answered.

"She wants to go to her husband," he translated, "but I told her we should wait right here."

Nate stood back so everyone could file in. He began reloading the Hawken, his gaze happening to fall on Samson. The mongrel was a yard off, staring intently down the corridor. Nate did the same, and felt his scalp prickle on beholding a bounding bunch of indistinct figures swarming toward them. "Here they come!" he shouted, his fingers flying, desperately striving to finish loading before the warriors reached them.

Shakespeare gave Zach a shove, propelling the boy into the bedroom. Then he faced their wives, both of whom were standing with their feet firmly planted and their features as hard as iron. "Blue Water Woman," Shakespeare bellowed, "you and Winona get in there and lock the door! We'll hold them off."

"No, husband," Blue Water Woman said. "Our place is with you."

There was no time to argue. Shakespeare slammed the door shut and turned to confront the onrushing Apaches.

As silent as a pack of marauding wolves, the warriors swept down the hall two abreast, the leaders with uplifted knives.

Nate rammed the patch and ball home, then yanked out the ramrod and let go of it rather than try to reinsert it. He whipped the Hawken up and cocked the hammer. Suddenly Winona and Blue Water Woman fired, dropping the first pair of Apaches. Nate sighted on one of the second pair and squeezed off his shot at the same instant Shakespeare did. The second pair toppled.

Then the rest were on them.

In a flash Nate leaped in front of the women and drew his loaded flintlock. A muscular warrior lunged at him. He sent a ball tearing into the man's chest, then tossed the useless flintlock down and reversed his grip on the Hawken to use it as a club.

To his right Shakespeare was grappling with a robust adversary while others tried to get past at the women.

Samson sprang at an attacker, his huge jaws closing on the warrior's throat.

A knife nicked Nate's left arm, and he slammed the rifle stock into the face of the warrior responsible. A younger warrior darted in close and tried to rip open Nate's abdomen. He just managed to deflect the blow, then smashed the stock into the Apache's mouth. But there was no respite. A pair of warriors sprang on him at once. Nate went down under their combined weight, jerking his head aside as a blade streaked past. A knee gouged into his stomach. Something else rammed into

his groin. His vision blurred. All around was confusion
as his wife and friends fought frantically for their lives.
Someone—a small girl?—screamed in mortal terror.
Samson was snarling fiercely.

"No!" Nate cried as a knife cut him in the side. He
heaved, throwing one of the warriors off, but the other
had snatched up his rifle and he saw the bloody stock
sweeping down. Again he jerked his head to the right,
but this time he failed to avoid the blow. Stars exploded
before his eyes. A numbing jolt jarred his chin. He struggled to recover his senses, to stand, yet he did no more
than touch an elbow to the floor when a great black wall
crashed on top of him. The last thing he heard was a
flurry of shots.

Someone was speaking in Spanish. The words were
fuzzy, as if his ears were plugged with cotton. He heard
the last one clearly, though. The word *"patron."*

A hand touched his shoulder. "Can you hear me,
señor?"

Nate opened his eyes, and blinked in the sudden brightness of a nearby lantern. He was lying on the floor, but
in the living room, not the hall, and next to him squatted
Francisco Gaona, a very different Gaona from the self-
possessed and confident host he had come to know and
respect. Francisco's face was almost colorless, his eyes
haunted by inner anguish.

"Thank God you have survived!"

"The others?" Nate asked, attempting to rise. Waves
of pain pounded his head and he sagged, momentarily
weak.

"Shakespeare is in a bedroom being tended to by one
of my servants. He was stabbed in the shoulder and the
neck. A *vaquero* is already on the way to Santa Fe for
the doctor."

"Our wives? The children?"

"Gone."

Pain or no pain, Nate pushed to his feet. He swayed, and Francisco held his arm until he steadied himself. "The Apaches took them?"

"*Sí*. And two other women who have served my family faithfully for many years."

Nate closed his eyes to ward off the tidal wave of despair that threatened to engulf him. Winona and Zach in the hands of Apaches! He might never see them again!

"Are you sure you should stand?" Francisco asked.

"I'm fine," Nate lied, straightening and staring at his devastated friend. He touched his own forehead and felt a large bump. On his chin was a nasty welt. His left side, where the knife had cut him, had stopped bleeding. The cut itself was no more than an inch or two long and not worth being bothered about. "How long was I out?" he asked.

"Perhaps fifteen minutes, no more."

The room was filled with bustling *vaqueros*, most disheveled, many grimy and sweaty, at least half sporting minor wounds. Those with more serious injuries were being treated by their friends. Others were loading guns. Some were preparing packs for travel.

"Tell me everything," Nate said.

Francisco stepped wearily to a chair and sat down. The picture of dejection, he touched a bruise on his cheek while watching the swirl of activity. "From what I can gather, there were twenty to twenty-five savages in the band. A few went after the horses in the corral, but I suspect this was a trick on their part to keep my *vaqueros* busy while the rest broke into the *hacienda*. They were after captives, not horses."

"They like to take prisoners?" Nate asked, thinking that his loved ones would be gruesomely tortured and left to rot somewhere in the vast wilderness.

"Not prisoners as such, *señor*. They like to steal women to be their wives and children they raise as their own."

The mental image of Winona being molested by a leering Apache made Nate's blood boil.

"I was out near the corral, helping my men, when I heard a great commotion inside and guessed what the devils were up to. Right away I came back in, but I was too late. You and Shakespeare were both down. My bedroom had been broken into and Apaches were dragging off our wives and the children. We shot some of the *bastardos*. The others used our wives as shields until they got out the back door. Then they vanished as Apaches always do."

"Samson?" Nate asked, expecting to learn that the dog had sacrificed itself in their defense.

"Your great *perro*? I did not see him anywhere, my friend. Not even his body."

"Would the Apaches have taken him?"

"I don't see why. They would have no use for him except perhaps as food, and they can find plenty of that whenever they want. Apaches are masters at living off the land."

Nate glanced at a *vaquero* who was stuffing a pack with jerked beef and bread. "You're getting set to go after them?"

"At first light we will give chase. Tracking them is next to impossible but we must try. We must track them down before they reach the mountains or our loved ones will be lost forever."

"Count me in."

"I was hoping you would say that. It is most unfortunate that Shakespeare is not fit to travel. We could use another skilled tracker."

"How many men are you taking?"

"Twenty," Francisco answered. He stared at a groaning, bloody *vaquero* lying on the floor and scowled. "I can't afford to take any more. Six of my men were killed. Four have been so gravely wounded that they will probably not live through another day. In addition, three of the servants were slain."

"At least we made the Apaches pay dearly."

"Did we? All we found was one dead savage."

"With all the firing your men did? And I know that we accounted for five or six of them in the hallway, maybe more."

"That is good to hear. But there is no way of knowing for sure how many were killed because Apaches don't like to leave their dead behind," Francisco said. He slowly stood and licked his dry lips. "This is all my fault. I should have posted more guards. But I wasn't expecting much trouble after dark. Apaches rarely raid at night. They'll steal horses and property, but they don't like to fight once the sun goes down. It has something to do with a belief that the spirits of those killed after dark will wander the earth instead of going on to the spirit land. Or so I was told."

Nate was touched by Gaona's feeling of guilt for what had happened. "You should get some rest before we head out," he recommended.

"Could *you* sleep at a time like this?"

"No," Nate admitted.

Their discussion was interrupted by the skilled *vaquero* named Ignacio, who entered the room, saw Nate, and came over bearing the Hawken and the flintlock Nate had tossed to the floor during the heat of the battle. He said something in Spanish and held the guns out.

"Ignacio believes these are yours," Francisco related.

"Thank him for me," Nate said, taking the weapons. He still had his other flintlock and his butcher knife, each wedged tight under his belt, leading him to comment,

"I'm surprised the Apaches didn't take all the guns they could lay their hands on."

"They have little use for guns since powder and ammunition are so hard for them to obtain," Francisco said. "And too, they can shoot arrows far faster than we can shoot our rifles and pistols, in many instances with much greater accuracy."

Nate was thankful the Apaches had seen fit to use knives instead of bows in the house, no doubt so their hands would be free for in-close fighting or for taking captives. That made him think of his wife and son. "I'd like to see Shakespeare. Which room is he in?"

"Ignacio will show you," Francisco replied, and gave instructions to that effect in Spanish.

The bedroom was at the middle of hall. An elderly woman admitted him, then politely stepped outside so he could be alone with the grizzled mountain man. McNair, flat on his back with his upper chest and neck heavily bandaged, looked up and mustered a lopsided grin.

"The next time I get a notion to go gallivanting around the country, shoot me."

Nate stared for a moment at the bright red stains on the bandages, then sat down on the edge of the bed. "Maybe you shouldn't do much talking. It looks like you've lost a lot of blood."

"I do feel a mite tuckered out," Shakespeare said. "Must be the worry. But it doesn't take much strength to flap my gums."

"We're going after them at dawn."

"Watch yourselves. They'll be expecting pursuit. You might wind up riding smack into an ambush."

"We'll do our best."

Shakespeare, wincing and grunting, shifted position. "Listen to me, son, and listen good. The lives of all those the Apaches took may wind up depending on you and you alone. Francisco is a good man, and his *vaqueros* are as brave as any I've ever met, but they're no match for Apaches out in the wild. They'll be out of their element.''

"Francisco says he has some good trackers.''

"By his standards they are. But they can't hold a candle to you or me, and they're babes in the woods compared to the Apaches.''

"It doesn't matter how good the Apaches are. I'm not letting those bloodthirsty sons of bitches get away.''

"That's nice to hear, but don't be so hard on them. They're only doing what comes naturally.''

"Did I just hear right?'' Nate asked. "How can you defend them after what they've done?''

"You don't know the whole story,'' Shakespeare said with a sigh. He draped a forearm across his clammy brow and elaborated. "The Apaches weren't always so hostile. When the first Spaniards showed up in this region the Indians hereabouts were downright friendly. Then the Spaniards took to enslaving them, to forcing them to work in the mines and the fields, to treating them as no better than animals. Their women were abused, their children left to starve.'' He paused. "How would you react if that happened to your people?''

Nate said nothing.

"Ever since then the Apaches have hated all outsiders. They waged war on the Spaniards and they're waging war on the Mexicans because the Apaches see them as intruders who have mistreated their people and taken over their land. Branding them as bloodthirsty is a pure and simple case of judging another people's corn by your own bushel.''

"I had no idea.''

"Now that I've said my piece, I have one thing left to add,'' Shakespeare declared, reaching out and grasping Nate's wrist. "Do whatever it takes to save our loved ones. Hound the war party to the ends of the earth if need be. Kill as many Apaches as stand in your way. But no matter what, *save them*.''

Nate simply nodded.

Weakened by his exertion, Shakespeare collapsed and closed his eyes. "So tired," he said feebly. "So tired." In moments he was sound asleep.

A long silence ensued as Nate sat and stared at his slumbering friend. At length he stood, gave McNair a pat on the leg, and hurried off to get dressed and load all his guns. Soon it would be morning, he reflected. Soon he must match wits with the fiercest warriors west of the Mississippi.

And all too soon he might well be dead.

Chapter Nine

They were a grim, determined group of men as they rode away from the *hacienda* before the sun even rose. A rapidly spreading golden tinge was brightening the eastern half of the sky and affording enough light for them to see the ground well enough to track the Apaches. From the southwest wafted a warm sluggish breeze promising a blisteringly hot day.

Nate rode at the front of the somber *vaqueros* between Francisco Gaona and Ignacio. Since they wanted to travel fast they were traveling light. Rather than slow all of them down by bringing along a string of pack animals, each *vaquero* had a small pack containing a meager food ration and extra ammunition tied securely behind his saddle.

A man named Pedro, the best tracker on the *rancho*, was a dozen yards in front of the main body, bending low to search for sign. The ground was relatively soft in the verdant valley so Pedro was having no trouble trailing the band, as yet. But once they reached the more arid hills and rocky mountains the chore would become extremely difficult if not almost impossible.

From what Nate could see as he scoured the soil ahead, the Apaches had made no effort to conceal the tracks left when they lit out with the captives and their spoils. While the *vaqueros* had prevented the war party from stealing any of the prize stock in the corral, the Apaches had taken some of the free-roaming horses and mules; a half dozen of the former and seven or eight of the latter. The hoof prints were as plain as the nose on his face.

He wondered about such apparent carelessness. From all he had heard about Apaches they *never* made mistakes. So why would they try to steal a small herd of stock when they knew the Mexicans would soon be in earnest pursuit, when they knew the tracks would lead the Mexicans right to them? There was only one answer as near as he could tell, which filled him with dread.

The tracks took them to the southwest, toward harsh, rugged country fit neither for man nor beast.

Within three hours they came to a narrow plain crisscrossed by shallow *arroyos* and deep ravines. Beyond lay a range of mountains, the peaks devoid of snow, thrusting stark and barren high into the dry air. Here Pedro slowed because reading the sign was much harder.

"It is too bad about the dust," Francisco abruptly commented. "They will see us coming from a long way off."

Preoccupied with his thoughts, Nate hadn't paid much attention to the body of *vaqueros* behind him. He now did, twisting to see the that a swirling cloud of dust was rising from under the hoofs of their many mounts. "You should string them out," he said.

"*Señor?*"

"Instead of riding all bunched up the way we are, you should have the *vaqueros* string out in a line with no more than two men riding side by side. We'll stir up less dust that way.''

Francisco seemed stunned by so obvious a suggestion. ''I should have thought of that myself, but I'm afraid that I am not thinking very clearly at the moment. I am too filled with worry. Do you realize that I know of only two times where women taken by the Apaches were ever recovered?''

''Then this will be the third,'' Nate said.

''I pray it is so, my friend,'' Francisco responded, and gave instructions in Spanish to Ignacio, who then slowed to mingle with the body of *vaqueros* and relay the orders. Presently they were strung out as Nate had advised, two abreast, and the telltale cloud of dust was drastically reduced.

The ground became harder, rockier. The hoofprints virtually disappeared. Several times Pedro held up a hand and called a halt; then he would dismount and get down on his knees to better check for sign.

While waiting, Nate would scour the ground himself, and he noticed that he was able to see nicks and scratches that Pedro apparently missed. At the third halt he turned to Francisco and commented, ''Maybe it would help matters if I gave Pedro a hand. Two sets of eyes are better than one.''

''Of course,'' Francisco said, and called out to Pedro.

Putting his heels to Pegasus, Nate joined the middle-aged tracker, who greeted him in Spanish, then gestured helplessly at the ground. This was the rockiest soil yet and there appeared to be no sign whatsoever. Nate stayed in the saddle and moved in a small circle, doubled over so he could search for smudges and other traces of the war party's passing. Seconds later he saw where a hoof had left the faintest of impressions, and he pointed it out to Pedro, who had to practically touch his nose to the rocky surface to see it.

Pedro glanced up, his expressive features betraying how impressed he was. Rising, he mounted and motioned for Nate to lead the way.

Now they moved much faster. Nate concentrated exclusively on the ground, tracking as would an Indian, noting spoor the average mountain man would miss. Which was understandable since he had been taught by Shakespeare McNair, whose tracking skills were legendary, and by some of the very best trackers in the entire Shoshone nation. Where other white men would see only a blank earthen slate, he saw a pattern of scratches and scrapes that plainly revealed the direction the Apaches had taken.

After a mile Pedro rode back and said something to Francisco that brought Gaona up to ride with them.

Nate hardly noticed, so intent was he on overtaking the band so he could free the captives. He did deduce that the trail was leading into a narrow notch between two of the mountains, and when he was a few hundred yards away he reined up.

"Is something wrong?" Francisco asked.

"I don't want to ride into an ambush," Nate said, pointing.

"It is an ideal spot," Francisco agreed. He waved an arm to bring the rest of his men forward. "But I see no way to go around. They have planned well."

"One of us should go on ahead and scout around."

"It would be suicide. They would kill him on sight."

"Maybe not. They wouldn't want to give us any advance warning. They might let a single rider go in and come back out without jumping him just so we'll think it's safe."

"You hope."

"There's only one way to find out for sure," Nate said, bringing Pegasus to a trot.

"Wait, *señor*!" Francisco cried.

But Nate merely gave a wave of his hand, hefted the Hawken, and rode straight for the mouth of the notch. The defile wasn't more than 20 yards wide. On the right was a gradual slope dotted with scrub trees. On the left was a steep stone face marred by countless cracks and fissures. The quiet was absolute; not so much as an insect buzzed.

Squaring his shoulders, Nate boldly advanced. The notch was in shadow, which was a welcome relief after he had been roasted by the blistering sun for so long, but it gave him an uneasy feeling. He swore he could feel hostile eyes on him every step of the way. Pegasus began acting skittish, confirming his hunch. Yet although he scoured the adjacent mountains intently, he saw nothing to show there were Apaches lurking in wait.

The notch curved at the middle, angling to the southwest. He stopped and looked back. Francisco and the *vaqueros* were still visible, but they wouldn't be once he rounded the curve. If he ran into trouble they wouldn't see it. He'd be on his own.

Gripping the reins tighter, he kept going. He tried to think like an Apache. If he was one of the band, where would he set up the ambush? Where else but right there? The *vaqueros* would be hemmed in by the slope and the cliff. And being halfway through the notch, they would have to run a gauntlet of arrows to get to safety at either end.

He scanned the cliff, then the slope. Even his keen eyes failed to detect tracks. Maybe he was wrong, he thought. Maybe the Apaches had gone on through and were miles off. Then he saw the dirt.

Five yards up on the slope to his left was a patch of bare earth bearing tiny lines that ran every which way. The lines were so faint that Pedro would never have spotted them. Clearly they were made by something rubbing back and forth across the patch. Lying a few feet from the spot was the answer: a handful of saxifrage that had been pulled out and used to erase the hoofprint or footprint that would have given the Apaches away.

Feigning a casual attitude, Nate stretched and gazed higher up on the slope. About 60 feet up was a sizeable group of large boulders, some as massive as a cabin, more than enough to conceal a dozen or so mules and horses. And captives.

He could have turned around. He could have left the defile without being harmed since he was right about the Apaches not wanting to alert the *vaqueros*. But he couldn't. Not when he knew with every atom of his being that his wife and son and Blue Water Woman and Maria and Juanita and the servants were right up there behind those boulders.

His next act took the Apaches completely by surprise. Call it stupidity. Call it brash recklessness. Call it a supreme act of human bravery. Whatever, Nate suddenly reined sharply to the left and raced right up the slope toward those boulders. He covered a dozen feet before the Apaches realized he knew they were there and guessed his intent.

A burly, swarthy figure popped up seemingly from out of the ground, directly in his path, and drew back a sinew bowstring.

Nate already had the Hawken to his shoulder. He fired before the warrior could, the ball catching the Apache in the chest, dropping him where he stood. Others materialized out of thin air like demonic wraiths from some nether realm. A shaft whizzed past his head. Another clipped his beaver hat.

He saw a powerful brave rise from behind a skimpy bush that wouldn't have hidden a rabbit. The man lifted a bow. Instantly Nate turned Pegasus ever so slightly, ramming into the Apache. The gelding's chest caught the warrior flush, sending him flying end over end.

Another arrow nicked his shoulder.

Then he was almost to the boulders, and he looked up to see a tall warrior about to leap from the top of one, a knife clutched in the man's bronzed right hand. His own right flashed to a flintlock, sweeping the pistol clear as the warrior sprang. In a blur he cocked the hammer and fired, and the Apache's nose splattered all over the man's face and the plummeting body missed the gelding by inches.

Below him the notch rocked to a flurry of gunshots. He didn't dare glance back to see what was going on because yet another Apache had stepped into view around a boulder. This one held a lance and he had it poised to throw. In a twinkling it was streaking at Nate. He ducked low and felt his hat swept from his head.

Then he was beside the warrior and leaning down to slam the flintlock into the man's face. The Apache's head snapped back, hitting the side of the boulder, and the man toppled.

"Pa! Pa! We're here!"

The cry electrified Nate. He raced around the boulder and saw them all: the horses, the mules, the servants, the Gaonas, Blue Water Woman, and those who meant more to him than life itself. The captives all had their wrists bound and were seated with their backs to the boulders, all except young Zach, who had leaped erect to shout and was now resisting the efforts of a sturdy warrior to shove him back down.

At the sound of Pegasus's hoofs the Apache let go of the boy and whirled, drawing a knife. Nate jumped down, jammed the spent pistol under his belt, and moved to draw his other flintlock. But he was too slow. The guard reached him in three prodigious bounds. Nate barely got the Hawken aloft in time to deflect the blade arcing downward. The force behind the blow knocked him backwards and he nearly lost his balance.

As stoically as if made of granite, the Apache closed, slashing wickedly, a swing that nearly ripped open Nate's stomach. He swung again, or began to, when suddenly he stumbled forward as if struck from behind.

Nate's heart leaped when he saw Zach behind the warrior, and he realized the boy had come to his rescue by kicking the Apache in the leg. The warrior coiled to lunge at Zach. Frantically Nate drew his pistol and without thinking shot the Apache in the back of the head.

All the captives were rising. Winona rushed toward him. From down on the slope came constant gunfire mixed with loud yells and fierce war whoops.

For the moment the area at the rear of the boulders was free of Apaches. Nate stepped to his son, his smile the only emotion he could show until they were safely in the clear. He jammed the second pistol under his belt, set down the rifle, and drew his butcher knife. In a thrice he had the boy cut loose, then he faced the others. "Hurry!" he said. "We'll take these horses and—"

"Pa!" Zach screamed, his wide-eyed gaze going over Nate's shoulder.

Nate tried to spin. He was halfway around when something smashed into the side of his head, knocking him sideways. The world swam, his knees buckled. He felt his brow hit the ground. Someone—Juanita?—screamed. He heard Zach yelling.

"No! No! Leave my ma be!"

Then he heard something else, a sound that froze his soul but galvanized him to grit his teeth and push up into a crouch. One of the stolen horses was in full flight up the slope, and mounted on it was a brawny Apache working the rope rein with one arm while holding Winona in the other.

Not again! Nate's mind shrieked. He shoved upright, aware of a sticky sensation where he had been struck, and stumbled toward Pegasus. As he lifted his foot to a stirrup his ears registered the drumming of heavy footfalls behind him. Pivoting, his vision still blurred, he extended the butcher knife.

"It's us, *señor*!"

Francisco and a dozen *vaqueros* poured around the boulder, immediately going to the assistance of the captives. Francisco himself dashed to his wife and daughter and tenderly embraced them.

Nate again began to mount, but a small hand touched his.

"Pa? You're hurt. Don't go yet."

"I've got to, son," Nate said, his head throbbing terribly.

"But you're bleeding bad. You should wait a bit."

"I have to save her," Nate said, finally getting his moccasin into the stirrup. He tried pulling himself into the saddle, but his traitorous head swam worse than before. Inadvertently, he groaned. Bitterly frustrated, he shook himself and tensed his legs. The next instant a strong arm looped around his waist and he was pulled away from the Palouse.

"No, my friend," Francisco said softly. "Your *hijo* is right. We must see how badly you are hurt before you go anywhere."

"They took her," Nate protested. He tried to pry Gaona's arm loose, but a firm hand gripped his wrist, stopping him. Ignacio was there, sadly shaking his head. Struggling to control his anger, knowing they were only trying to be helpful, Nate let them seat him on a flat rock. His vision abruptly cleared and he saw that the fleeing Apache and Winona had long since disappeared.

Only then did Nate learn another reason the Apaches had used the boulders for concealment. At the base of one was a small spring. A *vaquero* knelt there, soaking a strip of cotton he had torn from his own shirt. He gave it to Maria Gaona, who quickly wiped the blood off Nate's head.

"You have quite a gash, *señor*," Francisco said.

A sharp pang lanced Nate's skull and he winced. "It's nothing," he fibbed. "I'll be fit as a fiddle in no time."

"You took a great risk in what you did."

"It couldn't be helped," Nate replied. He felt Maria's slender fingers gently probing the wound. "But I sure am glad you showed up when you did."

"I was concerned for your safety. We came at a gallop the moment you vanished around the curve," Francisco stated. "By flushing the Apaches as you did, your shots forewarned us and gave us a fighting chance. Thankfully, we were able to drive them off." He shifted and stared to the southwest. "I am only sorry that our victory was not complete. If your wife was here all would be well."

"I'm not going back without her," Nate disclosed.

Francisco nodded. "I will send half of the men back to the *rancho* with the women and the children and the rest of us will go after her."

"No."

"No?"

"*I'll* save her. You'll need all of your men as escorts in case the Apaches regroup and try to stop you."

"Am I to understand you intend to go after your wife all by yourself?"

"Yes."

"I will not hear of it."

"What about your wife and daughter? Do you want to risk losing them again?" Nate asked, and saw anxiety flare in Francisco's eyes. "Of course you don't. So get them home as fast as you can and don't worry about me. I can go a lot faster and be a lot less conspicuous if I'm by myself. On Pegasus I have a good chance of overtaking the Apache who grabbed Winona well before nightfall."

Gaona frowned. "You are very persuasive. But I still do not like separating."

"If you won't do it for me, do it for Maria and Juanita," Nate said, and stood, unwilling to waste more precious time arguing. He gathered all his weapons and strode toward the Palouse, then halted. Zach and Blue Water Woman were next to the gelding, waiting. "I want you to go back with Francisco," he told his son. "Your ma and I will be along shortly."

"I'd rather go with you."

"Out of the question," Nate said, stepping over to grip the reins.

"I can help you."

"You'd only slow me down and give me twice as much to worry about," Nate declared, and promptly regretted doing so when Zach bowed his head, crestfallen. Squatting, Nate touched the boy's chin and tilted it upward until they were eye to eye. "I appreciate the offer. Any other time I might accept. But I need to ride like the wind if I'm to save your mother, and you know there's hardly a horse anywhere that can keep up with Pegasus." He paused. "Do you want to slow me down and give that Apache a chance to get away?"

"No," Zach answered contritely.

"Then do as I say. Go back. See if you can find out what happened to Samson."

"He's missing?"

"No one knows where he is. I half expected to find him trailing the band that took you, but I haven't seen hide nor hair of the ornery cuss," Nate said, trying his best to keep his tone lighthearted. "The last time I saw him was during the fight in the hallway."

"Me too."

"So we each have someone to find. I'll get your ma, you hunt down Samson."

Fired with a new purpose, Zach nodded vigorously. "You can count on me, Pa."

Nate leaned forward to give his son a hug and a kiss on the cheek. Rising, he saw that Blue Water Woman was staring expectantly at him. "Is anything wrong?" he inquired.

"Shakespeare?" she said, wringing her hands.

Insight brought a deep sense of guilt at his own neglect. He realized with a start that she had no idea what had happened to her husband and she must be tormented by apprehension. "He was stabbed twice. He's lost a lot of blood, but he's doing fine as near as I can tell. They've sent for a doctor from Santa Fe."

"I saw him go down," the Flathead said softly.

"What he needs most is you by his side," Nate said. He mounted, smiled at Zach, and nodded at Blue Water Woman. "You listen to her, you hear, son? Until we get back she'll look after you."

"I will, Pa."

Blue Water Woman gave Nate a meaningful look. "You need not worry. Your son will be our son until we see you again."

"Thank you. And be sure to tell that no-account husband of yours to quit loafing in bed. He does enough of that at home." Nate turned the Palouse, and was about to ride off when Francisco hurried up bearing one of the food packs.

"Take this, my friend. You might need it."

Inwardly chafing at every second of delay, Nate politely accepted the pack and secured it behind his saddle. Leaning down, he offered his right hand and said, "Just in case."

"May God go with you."

Finally Nate headed out, moving to where the fresh tracks of the Apache's mount led upward from the boulders. He followed them easily, and soon noticed that the left rear hoofprint bore evidence that the hoof itself was cracked, which was knowledge that might come in handy later should the Apache hook up with other mounted warriors. Since few horses went around with cracked hoofs, so distinctive an identifying mark would enable him to pick that horse out from any others.

He came to where the slope slanted westward. Drawing rein, he swiveled and looked down on the rescue party. Every single one of them was watching him, every man, woman, and child. Zach took a few steps and waved. His throat constricting, he waved back.

The breeze wafted the boy's yell toward the heavens. "Be careful, Pa! I love you!"

All Nate could do was wave again. He was afraid his voice would give him away if he shouted. For several seconds he lingered, burning the picture of his son into his memory. Then, facing front, he lashed the reins and galloped in lone pursuit of his wife and her wily, savage abductor, heading into the very heart of Apache country, into the very heart of a land no other white man had ever penetrated.

Chapter Ten

The mountain vastness of the Apaches was every bit as picturesque as the northern Rockies, but the harsh beauty was lost on Nate. He had eyes only for the tracks he followed. The trail took him ever deeper into the range, sometimes along animal trails where the going was easy, more often as not over rocky ground where reading the sign was supremely hard to do.

He didn't get the impression the warrior was in any great hurry. After the first mile the Apache had slowed his mount to a walk, evidently in the belief no one had given chase, and from there on the mount had been held to a leisurely pace.

Winona and the Apache were riding double, which upset Nate immensely. He didn't like to think of the Apache's hands on her body. But at least, he mused, she was safe as long as the Apache kept going. Not until they stopped would the warrior be able to have his way with her, if that was his intent.

The miles fell behind him. The sun climbed higher and higher. He was sweating more than he ever had before, and so was Pegasus. Late in the afternoon they were able to partially slake their thirst at another small spring nestled among rugged rock formations. The Apaches, it seemed, possessed an uncanny knack for finding water where none supposedly existed.

He saw wildlife here and there: several black-tailed deer, chipmunks, a coyote, and the ubiquitous rabbits. A hawk soared overhead for a while, perhaps studying him, and then flew on. At the lower elevations he saw some cactus and grama grass. Higher up grew scrub oak, piñon, and some ponderosa pine.

From the tracks he knew he was gaining on them, and he had every hope of spotting them when there was plenty of daylight left. He got his wish an hour before sunset, but under circumstances that compounded his fears for Winona's safety.

He was negotiating a switchback up a steep divide when he heard several whoops from the far side. Hurrying to the top, he hid behind a pine and surveyed the canyon below. To his consternation, the Apache he had been trailing had been joined by four tribesmen, and they were standing near the stolen horse talking excitedly. On the horse, her posture as defiantly erect as she could make it, sat Winona.

Nate's heart leaped out to her. He longed to spirit her away from there. But what could he do when the odds were so heavily against him? If he attacked when they were out in the open they'd see him coming from a long way off, and fill him with arrows before he got close enough to see the whites of their eyes.

His cause wasn't hopeless, though. The four newcomers were afoot, so if Winona's abductor wanted to stay with them he had to go at a much slower pace. Five minutes later the prediction was borne out when all five

Apaches hiked westward, the one who had snatched Winona leading the horse.

Nate never lost sight of them from then on. Using every available bit of cover, hanging far back to further reduce the risk, he dogged them until they made camp for the night in a gulch. He watched as they collected wood and made a fire. He observed two Apaches hasten off to the northeast, and was amazed when they returned within ten minutes bearing a slain deer.

Winona, much to his relief, was largely ignored. She sat by herself across the fire from the warriors. Every so often one or another of the men would try to engage her in conversation using sign language, but she always ignored them. Ignoring her captor proved impossible, however, when the buck was brought in. He marched up to her, hauled her to her feet, and through sign language directed her to cook their meal or he would cut off her ears.

From his hiding place in a dense thicket 30 yards from the camp Nate was able to make out what the warrior told her, and he tensed in nerve-tingling dread that she might refuse and be horribly mutilated. He held his breath until she moved her hands, signing she would comply. The Apaches settled down to talk and left her to carve up the buck.

Nate's stomach grumbled in protest when the heady scent of the roasting deer haunch was carried to his nostrils by the obliging breeze. He was famished, but he refused to eat until after he saved his wife.

Soon the Apaches were eating greedily, tearing into large pieces of meat with their fine white teeth, and occasionally wiping their greasy hands on their bronzed bodies.

All five were dressed similarly in that the lot of them wore breechcloths. Four of the five wore the distinctive style of high-topped moccasins unique to the Apaches, while the fifth went about barefoot. The long black hair of each man was parted in the middle and held in place by a headband. All five were armed with bows. One of them also had a lance.

And Nate finally had a good look at the weapon responsible for nearly splitting his head open earlier. Winona's captor had a stone-headed war club he carried wedged under a strip of leather wound around his muscular waist. Such clubs, Nate had heard, were often more deadly than tomahawks.

Once the Apaches finished their meal they sat around talking. The warrior who had grabbed Winona did most of it, leading Nate to surmise that he was telling about the raid on the Gaona *hacienda* and the subsequent battle in the defile.

Eventually, with the fire burning low, the Apaches retired by simply lying down where they were seated and going to sleep. Winona was bound hand and foot by her captor before he too turned in. Incredibly, they didn't bother to post a guard.

Nate couldn't believe his good fortune. They must be overconfident, he reasoned. Since no one had dared enter their country for so long, they considered attack unlikely. He bided his time, waiting until the fire was reduced to sputtering embers and all the Apaches were perfectly still before he inched out from his hiding place and crawled toward their camp.

He circled to the right, moving in a loop that would bring him around to the side of the fire where Winona lay. She was curled up with her back to the fire, her bound arms held close to her legs.

All the stories he had ever heard about Apaches went through his mind as he stealthily worked his way toward the woman he loved. It was claimed Apaches were men of iron resolve and constitution. They were able to cover 70 miles a day on foot without needing a single drop of water. When they wanted, they could vanish as if into thin air. They had the eyes of eagles and the ability to hear twigs snap a mile off.

Many of the tales were undoubtedly exaggerated. What bothered him was that at the core of every wildly embellished yarn was a kernel of truth. Apaches might not be the men of inhuman ability they were alleged to be, but there was no disputing they were among the finest warriors ever known. He must rely on all the skill he'd acquired if he hoped to effect the rescue.

He completed half of the circuit when the unexpected occurred. The stolen horse, which was tethered to the south of the fire, suddenly looked in his direction and nickered. Instantly flattening, he placed his face against his arm so the pale sheen of his white skin wouldn't stand out against the ebony backdrop of the night, and peeked over his wrist at the sleepers.

Only two of them were no longer sleeping. The Apache who had taken Winona and one other were both sitting up and gazing all around them. Both glanced at the horse, which had lowered its head and was nibbling at a patch of grass. They continued to probe the darkness for five minutes. Then, satisfied they were safe, they lay down again.

Nate stayed right where he was for almost half an hour. He wanted to be certain the pair were again sound asleep before going another foot. Now that those two had been unaccountably awakened, they would be more apt to jump up at the first unusual noise, no matter how slight. He must be especially careful from here on out.

He widened the circuit he was making to put more distance between the fire and himself. The horse appeared to be dozing, so he needn't fear in that regard. Winona still lay curled up in a ball. The fact that she hadn't even lifted her head when the horse whinnied indicated she might be asleep, although he would be surprised if she was. How could anyone sleep under such circumstances? he reflected. He knew he wouldn't be able to if the Apaches had caught him.

The time crawled by as if weighted with a ten-ton anchor. Nate's elbows and knees were sore when he stopped 15 feet from his wife and surveyed the sleeping figures yet again. The warriors seemed to be asleep. His nerves tingling, he edged nearer. Winona's long tresses were hanging over her face, obscuring her eyes. She wouldn't realize he was there until he touched her.

His eyes darted from Apache to Apache, constantly checking their postures for any hint that one was awake and aware of his presence. Ten feet separated him from the woman he loved. Then eight feet. Then five.

Suddenly an Apache grunted and rolled onto his back.

Freezing, Nate touched the rifle hammer and the trigger, prepared to try and slay them all rather than be thwarted when he was so close to freeing Winona. But the Apache was breathing regularly and deeply. Thus assured, he crawled another foot and reached out to touch Winona's shoulder, to shake her and to let her know he was there. As he did his roving gaze happened to fall on the horse, and he saw with a start that the animal was no longer dozing, that it was looking right at him again, and he intuitively knew the damn animal would neigh and give him away just as it had before.

The next moment it did.

This time three Apaches came instantly awake, two of them leaping to their feet and looking all about them.

Nate had nowhere to hide. He was caught out in the open, exposed and vulnerable. Only the fact that the fire had died out delayed his discovery for a second or two. In that span he saw Winona raise her head and their eyes briefly locked. Impulsively, he touched her shoulder. Then one of the Apaches bellowed and rushed at him with a drawn knife.

Twisting, Nate cocked the Hawken and fired when the warrior was almost upon him. The heavy gun boomed, the ball taking the Apache high in the chest and flipping him over. Even as the man went down, Nate was leaping up and backing away to give himself room to maneuver. In a flash he drew his right flintlock and leveled it, but there was no one to shoot.

The Apaches had disappeared into the night.

He paused, about to run to Winona and cut her loose when an arrow streaked out of the darkness and missed his head by an inch or less. He heard it buzz as it went by.

"Run, husband! Run!" Winona cried.

Under ordinary circumstances he would rather chop off an arm or a leg than desert his wife when she needed him the most, but now he had no choice, not with the Apaches liable to pick him off at any second. What good would he do her dead? Realizing he would be foolishly throwing his life away and consigning her to a fate worse than death if he stubbornly tried to fight it out, he reluctantly whirled and ran, shouting over his shoulder, "Don't fear! I'll be back!"

An inky form hurtled at him from the left.

Nate fired without aiming, the flintlock belching lead and smoke. The warrior twisted and fell, then quickly scrambled out of sight behind a nearby boulder. Behind him he heard one of the Apaches yelling, and off to the left was the patter of running feet. Looking, he saw no one.

Bending low, he skirted a tree and plunged into dry brush that crackled underfoot and caught at his buckskins. It was an obvious mistake. Stopping, he crouched and listened, hoping his pursuers hadn't located his position.

The hunter had become the hunted. He sank onto his hands and knees and worked his way forward until he was out of the brush. Turning to the left, he advanced until he came to a stunted pine. There, he halted to reload the Hawken and the pistol.

He was terribly upset. Everything that could go wrong had gone wrong. Now the Apaches knew he was on their trail, and should he be lucky enough to escape with his hide intact he would have to work twice as hard to free Winona since they would be on their guard at all times. All because of that lousy horse!

There was one small consolation. Quite by accident he was leading the Apaches away from Pegasus. Odds were they wouldn't find the Palouse, which was a blessing. If he was left afoot now, not only would any hope of rescuing Winona be gone, but his very survival would be at stake. A man needed a lot more water when on foot, which was more difficult to find since a man couldn't cover as much territory in search of it as a man on horseback. Nor could a stranded rider find game as readily. If the Apaches found Pegasus, Nate would be hard pressed to stick to their trail and still satisfy his hunger and his thirst.

The guns were loaded. With the Hawken in his left hand and the pistol in his right, he rose and warily hiked northward. The faintest noise was enough to make him as rigid as a tree until he felt safe enough to go on. Given all he knew about Apaches, he anticipated being transfixed or tackled at any moment.

Much to his amazement, he eventually worked his way around to where he had concealed Pegasus without incident. Mounting, he sat and pondered his next move. It would be wise, he reasoned, to seek high ground so he could spy on the camp come first light. Reining to the right, he had started to head for a rise when to the southwest he heard an almost inaudible sound that resembled for all the world the striking of a hoof against a rock.

Nate drew rein and gazed into the limitless gloom. A

troubling thought crept into his mind, a thought that blossomed into a certainty when the sound was repeated seconds later. Wheeling Pegasus, he galloped toward the Apache camp heedless of the noise he was making. If he was wrong he'd pay the price with his life. But if he was right—he had to know.

His hunch proved accurate. The Apaches were gone. Winona was gone. The warriors had taken their wounded or dead and lit out. Stunned, he stared at the remains of their fire and tried to make sense of their flight. Why would they run off when they outnumbered him? The most likely answer made him want to kick himself in the britches for not putting himself in their place and figuring out their next move in advance.

The Apaches had had no way of knowing how many enemies they faced. Since to their way of thinking no solitary white man would dare invade their mountain sanctuary, they must have figured there might be a large force closing in. Prudently, they had hastily departed with their captive.

Nate should have expected such behavior. Apaches, it was claimed, never attacked a larger opposing force unless they could do so from ambush with scant risk to themselves. They were raiders, first and foremost, men who preferred to strike fast and hard and then get out again before a counterattack could be launched. To the Apache way of thinking, a man who stole one horse without being caught or who killed an enemy without being wounded in return was a far better warrior than a man who stole 20 horses but who had to elude pursuers to do it or a man who killed five enemies but was wounded in the process.

Now he was stuck there until daylight. Tracking at night was next to impossible, and even if he could overtake them he didn't care to do so in the dark. Swinging down, he stripped off his saddle and saddle blanket and made himself comfortable. He was too overwrought to sleep but he had to try to sleep a little, if only so he'd be fully alert when he did catch up to them.

And catch up he would. To have been so close to Winona, to have touched her soft shoulder and gazed into her lovely, troubled eyes, had fanned the flames of love in his soul to a fever pitch. She was counting on him and he had let her down. But he wouldn't make the same mistake twice. The next time he would succeed!

His inner clock woke him when the eastern horizon was tinged with a pale pink glow. He sat straight up, surprised he had dozed off in the wee hours of the morning. The sleep had not done him much to relieve his fatigue, and his limbs felt sluggish as he stood and saddled the gelding. Swinging up, he rode in a southwesterly direction.

Now that the Apaches knew they were being followed they were doing their utmost to cover their sign. He went over a hundred yards before he found a partial hoofprint. Later on he found another. If not for the stolen horse, he mused, he wouldn't have a clue as to which way to go.

After the sun rose and he could see clearly he began to find small drops of blood here and there, which proved at least one of the Apaches was badly wounded. He suspected that he'd killed the warrior he'd shot with the Hawken, but he could be wrong.

His main worry was an ambush. One or two or all of the band might hole up somewhere until he came along and finish him off. Every tree, every boulder, every ravine might conceal a foe. His gut worked itself into a tight knot before he had gone a mile.

The morning dragged past. At noon it was blazing hot, and sweat caked his skin from head to toe. Shortly thereafter he came on the spring.

This was the largest so far, nestled in the shade of a bluff and ringed by grass. Although he burned with a

keen desire to press on after Winona, common sense
dictated he stop and rest, if not for himself then for the
Palouse. Wearily dismounting, he again removed the
saddle, then allowed the gelding to drink. Lying down,
he touched his own lips to the cool water and drank
greedily.

After their thirst was quenched he gave Pegasus a
rubdown using handfuls of grass. Then he let the horse
graze while he rested in the shade, occasionally dipping
his hand into the pool to sprinkle water on his face and
neck.

From the sign, he gathered that the Apaches had visited
the spring at daybreak, but had stayed only a short while
before hurrying on. The direction of their travel showed
they were continuing deeper into the mountains.

He tried not to dwell on the unnerving fact that he was
alone in the middle of a harsh land teeming with roving
bands of savage Apaches. Should he be slain, no one
would ever know exactly where or how he had met his
Maker. Winona might hear of his death from a bragging
warrior, but Shakespeare and Francisco would be left to
wonder and reflect on the widely acknowledged futility
of going against the dreaded Apaches on their own terms.

Presently he had Pegasus saddled and rode on. High
peaks reared on all sides like the foreboding towers of a
medieval fortress. The many boulders and rocky ground
reflected the heat back at him, presenting the illusion he
was riding through an enormous stone oven. Vegetation
was sparse.

The tracks led him on a winding course through gorges
and along dry washes, over ridges and around barren
peaks. Several times he discovered clear hoofprints, and
from the stride of the stolen horse, from the way it was
dragging its hoofs now and then, he knew the animal was
greatly fatigued. With ample cause, he decided. Its rest
last night had been interrupted, and it had been unable

to get a decent drink since the day before. Bearing Winona only added to its misery. How long, he wondered, could it hold out?

Nate thought of little Zach and how the boy would fare if a cruel fate made him an orphan. Shakespeare and Blue Water Woman would look after the child, Nate was sure. And under their guidance Zach would grow up to be someone his parents would be proud of. But Nate preferred to see Zach mature with his own eyes. There was no substitute for the first-hand joys of parenthood except the joys of marriage itself.

Mid-afternoon found him a thousand feet higher than he had been at the spring. The Apaches were steadily climbing. To where? Ahead lay massive ramparts shrouded in mystery.

He'd hoped to overtake the band before nightfall, which now appeared unlikely. Ceaselessly he scoured vantage points from which the Apaches might spy on him, but he saw nothing to show any were. Which proved nothing, since they were virtual ghosts when they wanted to be. They might know he was still after them; they might not. Regardless, he wasn't giving up.

By late afternoon a feeble but welcome cool breeze blew in from the northwest. He scaled a steep earthen slope and came out on top of a tableland covered with grass and dotted with trees, a virtual island in the midst of a sea of arid terrain, as unexpected as it was a joy to find. More so, for when he halted and scanned this oasis he spied a fair-sized lake off in the distance, its tranquil surface shimmering with the reflected radiance of the sun.

Were the Apaches here? he asked himself. The tableland was an ideal spot to stop for the night. For that matter, an Apache village might be situated close by. There was ample water for a large number of people, there was bound to be abundant game, and the isolated location made random discovery by outsiders unlikely. The place was perfect.

He must get under cover. Clucking the Palouse into motion, he rode to a stand of aspens, then slid down. His backside was sore, his spine stiff from all the time he'd spent in the saddle. He stretched to remove the kinks, tied the reins to a slender tree, and walked to the edge of the stand for another look-see.

To the north lay undisturbed wilderness. To the west, though, figures appeared, moving around the lakeshore. There were at least a dozen and they were all on foot.

Suddenly he detected movement much, much closer. He lowered his eyes to the southwest and inadvertently gasped on seeing a stout Apache approaching at a dogtrot. Instantly he ducked low, afraid he had been seen.

Behind the first warrior came others. Two, four, five, seven all told, strung out in single file as was Indian custom when a war party was on the prowl.

Nate huddled behind a screen of saplings and cocked the Hawken. Although none of the Apaches had made a sound, he was sure they'd spotted him. Why else were they heading directly toward the stand?

Chapter Eleven

Nate hesitated, torn between an urge to fight and an impulse to flee. He might be able to shoot three of the warriors before the group reached him, but the rest would swiftly overwhelm him. It was smarter in his estimation to make a run for it simply because Winona's future depended on his staying alive.

He had started to back away from the saplings when a remarkable thing happened; the Apaches veered to his left to bypass the stand entirely. A smile spread over his face as it dawned on him that they had no idea he was there. He heard them talking among themselves as they went by on the far side of the stand.

What if Pegasus whinnied? The anxious thought brought him to his feet and he quickly made his way to the Palouse's side. He need not have worried. The tired horse was standing quietly, dozing. Breathing a bit easier, he moved next to the east edge of the aspens. From this vantage point he could see the Apaches clearly as they trotted to the rim of the tableland and there stopped.

As he studied their features he was stunned to recognize one of them as a warrior who had been a member of the small band he had tangled with. He knew it was the same man from the green headband the man wore, which was the only green one he had seen on an Apache thus far.

He abruptly realized what they were up to, and gave inward thanks he'd reached the hidden oasis when he had. His earlier assumption that there was a village nearby must be correct. The small band had hastened there after the fight, and now one of them was leading reinforcements back to find him and kill him or capture him for later torture.

The seven warriors were standing less than 20 yards from the spot where he had come over the rim. If, for whatever reason, they went north instead of going down the earthen slope, they were bound to see Pegasus's hoofprints and they'd know their quarry was much closer than they believed.

Nate watched expectantly until, at a gesture from the warrior with the green headband, the entire group vanished over the rim. He sat back, elated. Then a jarring insight sobered him. If those Apaches made straight for the site of the fight, they might not see the tracks he'd left as he'd made his way to the tableland. But if they used the very same route he'd used, they'd find the tracks in no time and immediately turn around to come after him.

What should he do? Standing, he hurried to Pegasus, untied the reins, and swung up. He couldn't afford to take chances. Time was now more crucial than ever before. Finding and freeing Winona must be done rapidly.

He swung to the south, and stuck close to the ragged rim on the assumption he ran less risk of encountering

Apaches there than in the midst of their verdant Garden
of Eden. In this manner he covered over a mile.

Then he heard someone singing.

Nate instantly stopped and peered through the fir trees
in the direction from which the merry sound came. Beyond the firs was a meadow. Crossing it were four young
Apache women, all carrying baskets. They walked to the
east, to a stand of bushes, where two of them knelt and
commenced digging at the roots.

These were the first Apache women Nate had ever
beheld, and he scrutinized them with interest. They were
quite beautiful, what with their raven hair, smooth features, and decorated buckskin dresses. Being in their
twenties, they had yet to acquire the many wrinkles that
served as badges of distinction for older Indian women
who lived hard but rewarding lives in devotion to their
families.

They chatted gaily as they worked, feeling perfectly
safe in their mountain retreat. All four were soon digging,
and when their baskets were full of roots they rose and
hiked to the northwest.

Nate waited until they were out of sight. Dismounting,
he looped the reins around a low limb, gripped the
Hawken in his left hand, and padded after the four
women. He caught up with them in seconds, but kept
far enough back that his chances of being spotted were
remote. The women passed through a tract of trees, and
emerged on the south shore of the sparkling lake.

Now Nate laid eyes on a sight no other white man had
ever observed and lived to tell about. Spread out before
him was a large Apache village, which in one respect
was unlike any Indian village with which he was familiar.
The lodges were totally different from those of the Shoshones. In fact, they were totally different from those of
all the tribes living on the plains. Instead of dwellings
made from buffalo hides, the Apaches lived in structures

known as wickiups. Bowl-shaped, they were fashioned
from slender poles and then covered with grass and brush.

There were 40 wickiups along the lakeshore. Among
them played laughing, happy children. Women were engaged in a variety of tasks, everything from tanning hides
to constructing baskets. The warriors sat around talking,
sharpening knives, making bowstrings, or gambling.

Nate counted 27 men. The rest must be either out
hunting or on raids. He scoured the village from one end
to the other, but saw no sign of Winona. But he did spy
the stolen horse, tethered beside a wickiup close to the
lake. He settled down on his stomach and made himself
comfortable.

Soon, with the golden sun perched above the western
horizon, the women busied themselves preparing the evening meal. Cook fires were started. The children were
called from their play, and the men went to their respective wickiups to await their food.

At last Nate saw Winona. The warrior who had abducted her emerged from the wickiup next to the stolen
horse, turned, and motioned angrily. From inside came
Winona, who was grabbed by the arm and rudely shoved
to the ground. Through sign language the Apache ordered
her to fix his meal. Then he stalked off to a nearby
wickiup and began talking with another warrior.

As excited as Nate felt at seeing his beloved again, he
was more worried about her welfare. That she had an-
gered her captor was obvious. Why, he could guess. She
would not submit meekly to being mistreated. Winona
was a proud, strong-willed woman whose self-confidence
was boundless. And knowing her as well as he did, he
knew she would rather die than let herself be subjected
to the ultimate indignity.

Her captor must be finding that out for himself. What
would the man do next? Nate wondered. If the warrior
was a fool he would try to force himself on her and risk

having his eyes scratched out. Even if the man succeeded, he had to realize that at some point in the future, when least expected, he would wake up to find a knife buried in his throat.

Perhaps her captor was wiser than that. Perhaps he would take his time, try to seduce her gradually. If she eventually felt all hope of being rescued or escaping was lost, she might give in, if she didn't take her own life first.

A raging hatred burned in Nate's breast for the one who had taken her. He wanted to get his hands around the bastard's neck and squeeze, squeeze, squeeze until the Apache's tongue protruded and the man's face became as blue as that lake yonder.

Nate watched Winona cook the meal. Her captor returned, sat cross-legged, and ate without speaking. She took a small bowl and sat down several yards away, deliberately turning her back to him, which sparked an angry stare.

Keep it up! Nate wanted to shout, feeling a tight knot form in his throat. Swallowing hard, he scoured the entire village again, seeking evidence of dogs. The Shoshones and other tribes were partial to relying on dogs to guard their villages at night, so it was logical to expect the Apaches to do the same. Oddly enough, he didn't see a single one. Then he remembered being told by Shakespeare that the Apaches often *ate* dogs when other game was scarce, just like they ate horses and mules.

His stomach growled, reminding him of his own famished state. Steeling himself, he shut food from his mind and impatiently waited for the Apaches to retire. They seemed to take forever doing so. Once their meal was concluded, the women cleaned up while the men socialized. Parties of warriors gathered around various fires to discuss matters of importance.

As he lay there, an unusual and enlightening thought

occurred to Nate. For all their reputed ferociousness, the Apaches were much like every other Indian tribe. The men were born warriors, bred through countless generations to excel at warfare and raiding, and while they didn't count coup as did the tribes on the plains and those inhabiting the northern Rockies, they did take immense pride in their fighting ability. The women, like Indian women everywhere, lived what at first glance might appear to be lives of sheer drudgery, toiling from dawn to dusk at all the tasks necessary to feed and clothe their families, but they did so out of a sense of loving service, not because they were forced to. And the children were exactly the same as all carefree children everywhere, playing at the activities they saw the adults doing and hoping one day to be respected members of their people.

Viewing the Apaches as just another tribe gave him a whole new perspective. Yes, they were to be feared, but no more so than the Blackfeet or the Utes. Yes, the men were skilled warriors, but no more so in their way than the Shoshones or the Cheyennes or the Sioux were in theirs. The Apaches had adapted to the harsh land in which they lived just as the tribes living on the plains had adapted to the conditions there. Apaches were flesh and blood. They could be killed. They could be outfoxed. And he was going to prove it by freeing his wife from their clutches, by rescuing her from their very midst.

By the positions of the constellations the hour was nearly midnight when the last of the warriors turned in. The village lay serene under the myriad of shimmering stars. From the northwest came a strong wind, rustling the high grass and the leaves of the trees. Small waves rippled the surface of the lake.

Nate could wait no longer. Rising into a crouch, he stalked closer, his ears and eyes straining to their limits. From some of the dwellings came muffled snoring. Otherwise, all was as still as a cemetery. Near the first wickiups he paused and nervously licked his lips. Some of the entrances were covered with hide flaps or crude latticeworks, others weren't. Since he had no way of knowing if any of the Apaches were awake, he had to be careful not to walk past any doorways. A single warning shout would bring them all out like angry bees stirred from their hive.

He moved toward the wickiup by the lake, placing the soles of his moccasins down lightly with each step, wary of snapping a twig or causing a loose stone to roll. Close up, the wickiups were like great black turtles. Penetrating the darkness within each was impossible.

When he was halfway through the village he heard a grunt from a wickiup he was passing and halted, his scalp tingling until the grunt was replaced by low snoring. His palms slick, he crept past dwelling after dwelling until only one remained in front of him: the one where his wife was being held.

Suddenly he thought of the stolen horse. The animal was staring at him, but so far had made no sound. He tensed, dreading a whinny. A minute went by. Two. The horse lowered its head, disinterested. If he could, he would have given it a hug.

Nate leveled the Hawken and tiptoed toward the entrance. Suddenly something moved inside. In three quick bounds he was to the right of the opening, the Hawken upraised to bash out the brains of the warrior should the man step out. A heartbeat later someone did, only it wasn't the Apache.

It was Winona.

She backed out, her footfalls completely silent, and had begun to turn when she saw him. Her eyes widened and glistened as if from moisture. Her mouth forming a perfect oval, she threw herself into his arms and buried her face against his neck.

Nate smelled the scent of her hair and felt her warm

body pressed flush with his. He wanted to cry for joy, but he fought back the tears. Now was not the time, he told himself. Slowly he lowered the Hawken and gave Winona a fleeting embrace. Then he whispered in her ear, "Did you kill him?"

She shook her head no.

Too bad, Nate reflected. Taking her hand, he stepped to the bay and carefully reached down to untie the rope. The animal looked at him but made no noise. Moving to the lake, he turned to the right, hoping the soft lapping of the waves would cover the dull plodding of the bay's hoofs. Proceeding cautiously, they covered 50 yards without mishap. Then a hundred.

Winona was giving his hand such a squeeze that it hurt. She unexpectedly leaned against him and give him a kiss on the cheek. "I knew you would come, my husband," she whispered.

"I would never give up as long as I lived," Nate whispered back, and kissed her in return.

"I did not expect you so soon. I thought I would have to hide until the Apaches stopped looking for me, then try to find you."

"I was lucky," Nate said.

"Naiche knew you would show up too, but not tonight. He thought it would take you two or three days if Naretena did not get you." She paused, then elaborated. "Naretena and six others left this afternoon to hunt you down."

"I saw them," Nate whispered. "Who is Naiche?"

"The warrior who stole me. He was impressed by you, my husband, by the way you tracked us and fought them when you tried to save me. He said he had never known a white or Mexican who was a match for the Apaches, but you are."

"*He* said that?"

"In his way he is an honorable man."

Nate changed the subject. "Didn't he tie you tonight?"

"He did, but not as tightly as before." Winona grinned. "My teeth are as sharp as a beaver's."

By now they were well clear of the village and bearing to the south so Nate could reclaim Pegasus. He kept a vigilant watch on the wickiups, fearing the one called Naiche would awaken and discover Winona was missing. Truth to tell, he was surprised the warrior hadn't awakened when she snuck from the dwelling. Then he reminded himself that Naiche had just come back from a long, arduous raid during which the warrior must have gotten little rest. Secure in his own wickiup, Naiche must be sleeping as soundly as a hibernating bear.

"How are the others?" Winona asked.

"Francisco took Zach and Blue Water Woman back to the *hacienda*. Shakespeare was wounded but I expect him to pull through. He's as tough as a grizzly and three times as ornery."

"I feared you were dead until you showed up on the slope of that mountain, riding right into the trap the Apaches had set. Naiche said that what you did was one of the bravest acts he ever witnessed."

"It sounds like the two of you became fast friends," Nate commented testily, forgetting to whisper in his annoyance.

"I got to know him very well, my dearest," Winona said, relaxing her grip on his hand to rub her forefinger over his. "And I made it plain to him that you are the only man for me."

"Did he . . . ?" Nate began.

"He tried but his heart wasn't in it."

"No?"

"Apache men respect their women very much. They rarely hit them or mistreat them, even those they capture."

"They're regular saints," Nate muttered.

"Saints?" Winona repeated. "Oh. Now I remember the word." She laughed ever so lightly. "No, they are not saints. But they are men you would respect if you were not so jealous."

"Who's jealous?"

They fell silent, and presently reached the trees where Nate had left the Palouse. He stopped to survey the village one last time, then turned to go forward as a strident whoop rent the chill night air from somewhere near the lake. Seconds later there were more shouts and considerable commotion as roused Apaches spilled from their wickiups right and left.

"Hurry," Nate urged, giving the rope a sharp pull to hasten the stolen horse along. His own animal was right where he left it, and in moments both of them were mounted and moving slowly eastward so as not to make much noise.

"Naiche must have awakened and discovered I was gone," Winona commented quietly.

"Either that or one of them got up to heed nature's call and saw that the horse was missing, then woke Naiche," Nate said. From the uproar, the agitated Apaches were scouring the vicinity of their village for Winona. Soon, if they hadn't already, the warriors would fan out in all directions to try and find her.

"We should make a run for it," Winona recommended.

"I reckon," Nate said, although he had reservations. Once they broke into a gallop the enraged Apaches would hear them and give chase in force. With enough of a lead they could easily outdistance most of their pursuers, those on foot, but there had been several other horses in the village and they were cause for concern.

He poked his heels into the Palouse's flanks and angled

to the left, away from the rim, since a single misstep in the dark would plummet both horse and rider over the edge. Winona stayed at his side, her long hair flying.

Not 20 yards off there was a loud cry, echoed by another close behind him. More yells arose to the north.

Nate swallowed hard and leaned forward, making the outline of his body almost indistinguishable from that of Pegasus. Winona did likewise. It was an old Indian trick that rendered them less visible targets. At a gallop they crashed through brush and came out on an open stretch where he gave the gelding its head.

Suddenly a stocky figure materialized out of the shadowy murk, running to intercept them.

The Hawken was resting across Nate's thighs, the barrel pointing in the general direction of the Apache. It was a simple matter for Nate to swivel the rifle just so, cock the hammer, and fire without raising his body. The gun boomed, the warrior stumbled and fell. To their rear a chorus of shrill, bloodthirsty cries showed the Apaches were pursuing them in full force.

The thing Nate now dreaded most was that one of their animals would step into a rut or a hole or a wild creature's burrow and go down. The Apaches would be on them before they could mount double and continue their flight. Glancing over his shoulder, he saw a dozen or more ghostly shapes, all on foot but moving at an incredible speed. He'd heard tell that Apaches were some of the swiftest runners alive, and he was seeing that claim proved right before his eyes.

Still, the horses were faster and they began to pull ahead. He peered eastward, seeking some sign of the end of the tableland although he knew it was much too far off. A cluster of trees loomed in their path so he swung to the right, going around, then lashed Pegasus with the reins once they were in the open again. The bay, still fatigued from its long journey, began to flag, to drop back, forcing him to slow a bit to stay close to his wife.

With each passing moment the whoops of the warriors grew progressively fainter. He let himself relax a little, his confidence growing. Once they were in the maze of mountains bordering the Apache stronghold they would be safe. That is, if a roving war party didn't accidentally stumble on them.

At that instant a new sound was added to the frenzied racket to their rear, the sharp blast of a rifle.

Nate stiffened in dismay. He hadn't counted on the Apaches using guns, but he should have known better. Despite what he'd been told about the Apache preference for the bow and arrow, there were bound to have been warriors who, out of curiosity if for no other reason, had taken guns as part of their plunder from a raid and subsequently learned to use them.

"Husband," Winona suddenly said. "I think my horse has been hit."

He glanced at the bay, thinking she must be wrong because they were well out in front of the Apaches and the one who fired couldn't have seen them clearly. Odds were the warrior had tried to guess exactly where they were by the drumming of their mounts' hoofs, then fired blindly. Besides, he hadn't heard the bullet strike her horse. "Are you . . . ?" he began, and had to rein up sharply when the bay faltered and abruptly came to a stop.

Now that they were stopped, Nate could hear the stolen animal's heavy wheezing. Head sagging, it swayed. Quickly he moved Pegasus alongside it and held out his left arm. "Climb on," he directed.

Winona needed no encouragement, for now from behind them came the pounding rumble of pursuing horses, three or four at least. Her hand shot out and grasped his forearm.

With a surge of his powerful muscles, Nate pulled her up behind him. Her arms encircled his waist, her body molded flush with his. "Hang tight," he breathed, goading the Palouse into a gallop once more. Every second counted. The delay had proven costly, judging by the proximity of the horses after them.

War whoops confirmed the Apaches were close on their heels.

An arrow cleaved the air, missing Nate's head by a foot, but he paid it no mind. Fear for Winona eclipsed all else since she was more likely to be hit than he was. And he dared not ride a zigzag pattern to make aiming harder for the Apaches because doing so might enable the warriors to overtake Pegasus.

It was a furious race for life, with Nate keenly aware that both of their lives depended on the Palouse's performance. If the gelding faltered they were as good as dead. Or *he* was, anyway. Winona would wind up back in the clutches of Naiche.

He touched a flintlock, but decided against drawing it. Trying to shoot a gun accurately while astride the back of a moving horse was difficult under the best of circumstances. At night, at full speed, it would be a miracle if he scored a hit.

For the remainder of his life he would vividly remember those harrowing moments when fear dominated his being. Slowly, Pegasus increased the gap between them and the Apaches. The warrior armed with a rifle fired again, but this time he missed.

So intently was Nate concentrating on their pursuers that he was startled when suddenly a vast chasm seemed to materialize right in front of them. Too late he realized it wasn't a chasm at all. It was the earthen slope he had scaled to reach the tableland, but it might as well be a chasm because the very next second Pegasus plunged over the edge with a panicked whinny.

Chapter Twelve

They went down the steep slope on the fly, the gelding frantically digging its hind legs into the loose earth and then sinking down onto its rump as their momentum threatened to send them toppling end over end. A swirling gray cloud of dust enveloped them and spewed out to their rear.

Nate had to strain against the stirrups to keep from being unhorsed. One hand holding the reins and the Hawken, the other grasping Winona's arm, he barely stayed upright. The stinging dust got into his eyes and nose, and for harried seconds he couldn't see more than a yard ahead.

Somehow Pegasus saw they were near the bottom and gave a bound that brought them safely off the slope. In response to Nate's urging the Palouse raced off down a winding gorge, its hoofs ringing on the stony ground.

Were the Apaches still after them? Nate wondered. He looked back and spied a billowing dust cloud sweeping down the incline. The cloud parted enough to give him a glimpse of a single strapping warrior at its center. Apparently the rest had stopped at the rim, but for how long? He must lose this one Apache so they could make their escape.

Riding flat out over mountainous terrain in the dead of night is an unnerving experience at any time. Now, with the specter of a savage warrior close behind them and hot for his blood, Nate rode with his heart in his throat. The twists and turns of the high gorge slowed Pegasus down, allowing the Apache to keep them in sight most of the time.

What he wouldn't give for a level plain where the gelding could really move! But Nate knew that even Pegasus had limits. Eventually the Palouse would tire, giving the Apache the opportunity needed to overtake them. He must do something to stop the warrior and he must do it soon.

Around the next corner the gorge widened. Huge boulders dotted the ground. Nate cut Pegasus in behind one and reined up, then drew a flintlock. He didn't have long to wait. In the time it would have taken him to count to ten the Apache's mount clattered around the bend and swept abreast of the boulder. Nate promptly fired, rushing his shot. To his horror, he shot low.

The ball struck the Apache's horse, eliciting a terrified squeal, and the animal tumbled, its front legs buckling, sending the rider sailing. Arms out flung, the airborne Apache smashed with a sickening crunch into another boulder, then fell limp.

Nate couldn't wait to see if the warrior was truly dead. Others just might be coming. He rode on down through the gorge and out into the open. For the next hour he picked his way to the northwest. At last, positive they had eluded the Apaches, he wended into the middle of a tract of timber at the base of a flat-topped mountain.

There, as he suspected he might because of the trees, he found water in the form of an oval pool.

"You did it!" Winona said, touching her soft lips to the side of his neck.

"Pegasus pulled our fat out of the fire, not me," Nate wearily told her, and gave her a hand down. He swung his sore body to the ground, then stood aside as the Palouse stepped to the water to drink.

"Do you think they will find us?"

"Not if we're mighty careful," Nate responded. "At dawn we'll head for the *rancho*. If we keep alert we might make it back without any more trouble."

"You don't sound very confident."

"There must be thousands of Apaches in these mountains. Eluding them won't be easy."

"If anyone can do it, you can, my husband," Winona declared, stepping into his arms. They hugged and kissed. Then she rested her head on his shoulder and sighed contentedly. "No matter what happens, we are together again."

"As we'll always be."

He took her hand and walked over to the pool. Together they quenched their thirst. As much as he wanted to lie down and rest, first he stripped his saddle from the gelding, then reloaded the Hawken and the flintlock. "Sorry we can't have a fire," he remarked.

"I understand," Winona said.

They reclined on their backs on soft grass, linked their arms, and snuggled against each other. Nate thought of how close he had come to losing her, and uttered a silent prayer of thanksgiving for her deliverance. Somewhere in the wilderness an owl hooted. Elsewhere a coyote yipped and was answered by another. His eyelids became heavy and he had to shake himself to stay awake.

The gentle fluttering of warm breath against his ear caused him to look at Winona. He was amused to see she had fallen asleep so soon. Her ordeal had caught up with her, and after so many hours of uncertainty and peril she was resting peacefully at last. He lightly touched his lips to hers, then did the same to the tip of her smooth nose.

Feeling he must be the most fortunate soul on the face of the planet, he at length permitted sleep to claim him.

A low nicker from Pegasus brought Nate up in a flash. He stood still, listening, surprised to see the crown of the sun visible through the trees to the east. They had slept too long! They should have ridden out at first light!

Appalled at his oversight, he grabbed the Hawken and worked his way through the timber until he could view the land they had covered the night before. The three figures on horseback were over a mile off but there was no mistaking their identity. Apaches hounding their trail.

Back he ran to Winona. Shaking her gently, he said as soon as her eyes opened, "They're still after us. We have to push on."

Wordlessly she nodded, rose, and moved into the bushes.

Pegasus was saddled and Nate was mounted when Winona rejoined him. Sticking close to the base of the mountain, he rode until they were out of the high timber. A ridge afforded a convenient perch from which to check their back trail. There was no sign of the three warriors. By then, he reasoned, they were in the trees, close to the pool.

Since the Palouse was rested Nate had no qualms about pushing the horse for the next several miles. He wanted to get and keep a substantial lead, the more the better. In the meantime he had to do everything in his power to shake the doggedly tenacious trio.

For the life of him he couldn't figure out how the Apaches had tracked them so far. He's done his best to leave as few tracks as possible, but apparently all his efforts had been in vain. Or were the three warriors from another village? Maybe, he speculated, they had simply stumbled on the gelding's fresh tracks and decided to investigate.

Winona put her cheek on his back and kept it there for the longest while. She was strangely quiet, perhaps melancholy over being forced yet again to flee for their lives.

As the sun steadily climbed so did the temperature. It would be another unseasonably hot day, taxing the Palouse's strength even further. Nate wished he could stop every so often so the gelding wouldn't bake. Now and then he did pause for a couple of minutes, but it wasn't enough. Pegasus became caked thick with sweat.

When the blazing orb dominating the heavens was directly overhead, he halted in the shade of a cliff to give the Palouse an extended rest, whether it was wise or not. There was no water, no grass handy to rub the animal down. All he could do was loosen the saddle and stroke its neck.

"We must find more water soon," Winona remarked.

"First we have to shake these Apaches off our trail," Nate said. "Until then we can't take the time to hunt for water." He scanned the land they had just covered, but there was no trace of the warriors—yet.

"We could give them a taste of their own medicine and set up an ambush," Winona proposed.

"No."

"Give me a pistol, husband. Two of them will be dead before they know what is happening. The last will be easy to kill."

"No."

"Why not? The idea is a good one."

Nate looked at her. "It's too dangerous. We'd have to let them get too close. If they suspect what we're up to, if something gives us away, they'll take cover and we'll be in for the fight of our lives.''

"The real truth is that you are afraid harm will come to me.''

Her blunt assertion caught him flat-footed. Nate stroked Pegasus a few times before saying, "Can you blame me? I nearly lost you once on this trip of ours, and I'm not about to risk losing you again.''

"We must make a stand eventually," Winona said.

"We'll see. If I become convinced we can't outrun them, then we'll pick our spot and fight. Until that time, we keep going.''

"As you wish, husband," Winona responded, although she did not sound pleased.

For half an hour Nate stayed there in the shade, giving Pegasus a chance to cool down and recover somewhat. Finally he climbed up and extended his arm to Winona. In minutes they were riding hard to the northeast.

On a rim of caprock that afforded a panoramic view for miles in all directions, Nate reined up. A frown creased his mouth when he spied the three Apaches nearing the spot where they had stopped to rest. "Damn," he muttered.

"Do we ambush them now?''

"No," he said testily.

"As you wish.''

A bench took them to a lone peak. Once past the mountain they found themselves in a twisting series of canyons and draws. Far ahead appeared a divide at the center of which was a slender gap.

Nate was doing some serious pondering. Deep down he knew his wife was right; the only way they were going to shake the Apaches was by killing them. And if that gap should be what he thought it was—a pass to the other side of the divide—it might be just the place to hunker down and spring their trap.

He had to search some to find a relatively easy way to the top. In most spots the slopes were much too steep for the fatigued gelding. By using good judgment and climbing carefully he got them to the crown of the divide. Stopping, he twisted and saw the Apaches far below. The warriors had seen them and were coming on fast.

Nate entered the gap, which was no more than 40 feet wide and flanked by sheer stone walls impossible for a human being to scale. Three-quarters of the way through he found a crack large enough to accommodate a single person in the left-hand wall. Above the crack was a projecting ledge more than wide enough for someone to lie on. Here he halted.

"*Now* do we ambush them?" Winona asked.

"Yes."

"As you wish," she said impishly.

He rode on to the opposite end of the gap to confirm it was indeed a pass. From a spacious shelf he gazed down on a sprawling vista of spectacular mountainous landscape. Descending would pose no problem thanks to a game trail. "Here's where we leave Pegasus," he said.

Ground-hitching the gelding, they hurried back to the crack. Nate glanced up at the ledge, then stepped close to the wall, set the rifle down, and cupped his brawny hands. "Up you go."

Winona hesitated. "How will you get up there?"

"I won't. I'm hiding in the crack."

"Down here you will be at their mercy. Why expose yourself when there is enough room on the ledge for two people?"

"Now who's afraid?" Nate couldn't resist asking, and motioned with his hands. "Come on. You're wasting time. They'll be here soon."

Her displeasure transparent, Winona put her right foot in his upturned palms, tensed her legs, and surged upward when he gave her a boost. She easily caught the edge of the ledge and successfully pulled herself onto it. Turning, she lowered her hand.

"Take these," Nate said, holding up both the Hawken and one of the flintlocks.

Winona took only the rifle.

"This too," Nate prompted, wagging the pistol.

"You keep it. You will need it more than I will."

"I'll still have one flintlock, my knife, and my tomahawk. Take it. Please."

Winona made no answer. Instead, she positioned herself on the ledge so that she couldn't be observed from below.

"Contrary female," Nate muttered as he drew his other pistol. Easing into the crack as far as he could go, he held the guns at his sides and cocked both hammers. He was concealed well enough that a rider passing by would be unable to see him until the man was directly abreast of the crack.

Now came the hard part, waiting for the Apaches to appear and hoping against hope the warriors would think the two of them had gone all the way through the gap. The rocky ground helped since their footprints wouldn't show. Only Pegasus had left even partial tracks, which might deceive the Apaches.

Might, Nate reflected bitterly. He was realistic enough to fully appreciate that the Apaches hadn't garnered their justly deserved reputations as outstanding fighting men by foolishly riding into enemy traps. Another cause for worry was that some Apaches had undoubtedly developed the same uncanny sense of detecting impending danger he'd seen exhibited by several of his Shoshone friends and others. Men who lived in the world often acquired instincts the equal of the savage beasts with which they contended for mastery of the land, and snaring such men was often as hard to do as snaring a panther.

Beads of sweat formed on his brow and his palms felt clammy. No air got into the crack, so although the floor of the gap was in near constant shade it was still stifling in the confined space. Repeatedly he shifted the bulk of his weight from one foot to the other.

His thoughts strayed. Were Zach and Blue Water Woman back safe and sound at the *hacienda* by now, or had Francisco run into more Apaches along the way? What about Shakespeare? Did the doctor arrive in time to put the mountain man on the mend? And then there was Samson. The mangy mongrel had been part of the family for years. Zach would be devastated if it wasn't found.

Suddenly the awful quiet was broken by the sharp crack of a heavy hoof on a stone.

Nate broke out in gooseflesh. He lightly touched his fingers to the triggers of both pistols and girded himself for the fight. Speed would be the deciding factor. If things went as he planned, between Winona's rifle and his two flintlocks they would dispatch all three warriors with a single shot apiece. The Apaches would have no time to react.

The rattling of hoofs grew louder and louder. A horse snorted, perhaps having caught the Palouse's lingering scent.

Nate, through sheer will, calmed his jittery nerves. The Apaches were close, so close he heard words spoken softly in their tongue. Then there was a grunt, a single harsh exclamation, and total silence. The trio had stopped! he realized, his eyes glued to the section of the gap he could see. Why? Had they spotted Winona? Or were they so adept at reading sign that they knew he was in the crack? Dreadful uncertainty gnawed at him like a rat through cheese. He could barely stand the suspense.

Then he heard a peculiar sound, a sort of sibilant

hissing not unlike the noise made by steam escaping from a kettle. Cocking his head, he tried to identify what it could be. When he did, he nearly laughed aloud.

Soon the sound stopped, and the Apache must have remounted because the horses started forward.

Now Nate saw the brown nose of the foremost mount come into view. The head was next. Taking a breath, he took two bounds, bursting from the crack with his arms sweeping up even as from above him the Hawken thundered and one of the warriors was smashed to the ground by an invisible fist. He took a hasty bead on a second Apache and fired, but at the instant he squeezed the trigger the warrior began to lift a bow and his shot struck the man's arm, not the chest as he'd intended. The Apache jerked at the impact but didn't go down.

Venting a whoop in rage, the third warrior prodded his horse into a run and bore down on Nate with a war club raised on high.

Nate shifted and took aim, confident he would drop the man, and equally sure that if by some fluke he didn't, Winona would do the job. Then a thought hit him with the force of a bullet and made him blink in surprise. He'd forgotten to give Winona extra black powder and ammunition! Her rifle was now useless!

The oversight so distracted him that the onrushing Apache was almost upon him before he squeezed off his shot. A red hole appeared on the warrior's cheek and the man went down in a whirl of flying limbs. Nate had to leap out of the way of the Apache's charging horse, and he didn't entirely succeed. The animal clipped his left shoulder as it pounded past, sending him to his knees, and in the process jarring his left hand so badly that his unused flintlock went sailing.

"Husband!" Winona yelled.

He looked up to find the wounded Apache on the attack, galloping straight at him, hatred etching the warrior's swarthy face, a face he now recognized as being that of the man who had abducted his wife, none other than the Apache name Naiche. Releasing his spent pistol, Nate whipped his knife from its beaded sheath and pushed to his feet.

Naiche had let his bow fall. He appeared unfazed by his wound as, with both arms flailing, he tried to bowl Natc over. At the last instant Nate jumped out of the animal's path, then whirled to meet the next rush. Exhibiting superb horsemanship, Naiche wheeled his mount on the head of a pin and tried once again.

Nate frantically backed away, and felt his left heel bump an object lying on the ground. He tripped, falling backwards, and rather than fight gravity and be a sitting duck for Naiche he went with the fall, landing hard on his shoulder blades but quickly rolling to the right out of harm's way. Driving hoofs flashed on by.

Rising again, he saw that he'd tripped over the body of the first warrior he'd shot. Ten feet away lay one of the flintlocks, but was it the one he had fired or the other one? He started toward the gun, then stopped. Naiche was swooping down on him like a great painted bird of prey, trying to run him over. He feinted to the right, taking only two swift steps before reversing direction and darting to the left. His ruse worked. Naiche had angled his mount to compensate for the move to the right and was unable to swing it back before going past.

Swiftly Nate ran to the flintlock, grabbed it, and pointed the weapon at the Apache. Naiche didn't seem to care. Snarling, the warrior closed for the fourth time. Nate smiled in hopeful triumph as he cocked the pistol, but his expression was transformed into one of frustration when the hammer made a loud click and the flintlock didn't fire.

Naiche drew a large knife. He leaned down and lunged, lancing the blade at Nate's head, and Nate ducked down, narrowly evading the blow. Spinning, Nate did the unexpected. Instead of tiring himself trying to avoid the horse, he went on the offensive, dashing after the animal and leaping as Naiche, unaware of the bold gambit, was about to turn his mount for one more charge.

Nate's left arm closed around the Apache's waist and with his other he attempted to drive the knife into Naiche's side as the two of them began to fall. Somehow, Naiche blocked the swing. They landed next to each other, but promptly shoved apart and stood, each still holding his weapon.

For a moment they stood stock still, taking one another's measure. The Apache's eyes burned with inner fire as he contemptuously regarded Nate.

For Nate's part, he was noticing Naiche's exceptionally muscular build and the many scars on the warrior's body that bore eloquent testimony to the man's fighting prowess. Naiche was shorter but broader across the shoulders and hips, resembling a young grizzly in build.

The Apache struck with the speed of a striking rattler, his right arm flicking out at Nate's throat. Nate retreated a stride and countered with a slash at the warrior's stomach, but Naiche stepped to the left. Then they slowly circled, both seeking an opening.

Nate thrust out at chest height. The moment his arm was fully extended he arced the knife down lower, trying to slice open the Apache's stomach. Naiche twisted and the blade missed him by a fraction. Before Nate could regain his balance, the warrior lashed out, the blade of his knife striking the blade of Nate's so hard that Nate's arm was battered aside.

For a second Nate was wide open and Naiche promptly pounced, his left hand clamping on Nate's throat as his left knee slammed into Nate's groin. Together they went down, the Apache on top. Nate saw the tip of the warrior's knife sweeping at his face and he desperately wrenched his head aside. The blade nicked his ear, drawing blood.

Instantly Naiche raised the knife for another try. Nate bucked, striving to unseat his foe, but Naiche's knees pinned him in place. His own blade bit into the Apache's knife arm, not deep but inflicting enough pain to cause Naiche to jump up and take a bound to the right, out of range.

Nate rolled to the left, away from the warrior, and had started to rise when a foot caught him in the ribs, doubling him over. A second blow to the head knocked him flat. Dazed, he shifted, trying to stand, and glimpsed Naiche as the warrior leaped onto his back, pinning him again. He felt his hair gripped by iron fingers, and winced as his head was brutally bent backwards, exposing his throat to the Apache's blade.

Naiche gave a curt laugh that sounded more like a bark and went for the kill.

Chapter Thirteen

Nate stiffened as the terrifying realization that in another few seconds he was going to die coursed through him. He was totally at the Apache's mercy. There was nothing he could do to forestall the inevitable, but he refused to submit meekly. He reached up and tried to grasp the hand holding his hair to pry it loose even as he heaved his body upward with all the power in his legs and thighs.

Neither move accomplished a thing. His arm was swatted aside as casually as he would swat a fly, and the weight of the warrior combined with his own dazed state to prevent him from bucking Naiche off.

He struggled to pull his head down, to tuck his chin against his neck so the Apache would be unable to slit his throat from ear to ear, but couldn't. At any instant he expected to feel the cold steel slice into his soft flesh.

Then Nate heard a loud thump and the grip on nis hair slackened. Naiche unaccountably sagged to one side. Seizing the advantage while it lasted, Nate strained with all his might and threw the Apache off him. In the blink of an eye he had scrambled to his knees and turned to face his enemy.

Naiche was also on his knees and shaking his head to clear it. In the middle of his forehead was a nasty gash several inches long from which blood flowed down over his nose. The warrior still held his knife, but loosely in his lap.

For tense seconds neither of them moved as they both mustered their reserve of stamina. At first Nate didn't understand what had saved him, not until he saw his Hawken lying on the ground a foot away. He didn't need to look up at the ledge to know the answer. Winona had hurled the rifle at the Apache just as the warrior was on the verge of stabbing him, and the heavy gun had stunned Naiche.

"Behind you!" she suddenly shouted.

Nate rose unsteadily into a crouch and twisted. A few yards off was one of his flintlocks. But was it the one he had already fired or the loaded pistol? He'd dropped the useless one again and had no idea whether this was it. The swirling fight had jumbled his sense of direction so badly that he'd had no idea they were under the ledge until just now.

Naiche also stood, his baleful eyes virtual slits as he uttered a few stern words in the Apache tongue.

A threat, Nate figured, or a vow to kill him no matter what. He looked at the warrior, then at the flintlock, gauging whether he could reach the pistol before the Apache reached him. Since there was only one way to find out, and since any delay would give Naiche time to recover, he took a swift step and dived with his left hand outstretched. Behind him footsteps pounded and something stung his left leg.

Nate landed with a jarring thud on his stomach. His hand closed on the pistol and he whipped around to take aim. But Naiche was already on him, straddling his legs, and the Apache knocked the gun to one side. He saw the warrior tense to stab downward, and in that instant when Naiche was concentrating on the gun and Naiche's torso was unprotected, Nate streaked his right hand up and in, sinking his blade to the hilt in Naiche's stomach. Without pause he bunched his shoulders, then drove the knife to the right and the left, ripping the Apache's abdomen wide open.

Naiche staggered backwards, his features ashen, and pressed a hand to his intestines as they spilled out of the rupture. He blinked, looked at Nate, and said something. Then his legs gave out as all his strength drained from him like water from a sieve. He lifted his face to the sky, voiced a piercing cry, and pitched over.

Nate had to scramble to get out of the way of the falling body. He sat up, staring at Naiche's blank eyes. A spreading pool of blood and foul intestinal juices was forming under the warrior and rapidly spreading outward. Abruptly nauseous, Nate got to his feet and shuffled to one side.

"Husband?" Winona said softly.

Turning, he met her anxious gaze. "I'm fine," he said softly, his voice oddly hoarse.

"You're bleeding."

That he was. In several places. But none of the wounds were life-threatening. "They don't hurt much," he mumbled, and inhaled deeply. "I'll be all right in no time."

"Help me down."

He wiped his knife clean on Naiche's leg first and stuck the blade back in its sheath. Moving closer to the rock wall, he positioned himself so that his shoulders were directly under the edge of the ledge. "Lower away," he prompted, lifting his hands overhead. She dangled her legs and he caught them and braced her feet on his shoulders. Then, ever so carefully, she climbed down using him as a ladder. Once her feet were on the ground she embraced him and locked her lips on his and for the longest time there was no sound or movement in the gap.

Winona went for Pegasus while Nate reclaimed his weapons and reloaded his guns. A close examination showed the Hawken to be intact. He sat down, his back to the wall, and gratefully let Winona clean and dress his wounds. As she closed the parfleche and began to stand, he gently took hold of her wrist and said in his best Shoshone, "You are pressed to my heart forever."

She smiled and responded, "And you to mine."

Two of the Apache mounts had run off. Nate mounted Pegasus and easily caught the third one, which Winona then climbed on. Together they rode out the far end of the gap into bright sunshine and a warm breeze that Nate found refreshing. He surveyed the beautiful but uncompromising land below and nodded, glad to be alive.

For the remainder of the day they pushed on toward the Gaona *rancho*. Twice they came on Apache sign, but the tracks were days old. Evening saw them camped beside a trickle of a stream that had satisfied their thirst and renewed their vigor.

Nate listened to their small crackling fire and held Winona tight as he stared at the stars filling the wide expanse of sky. He thought about the nature of love, and how men and women would do anything, including putting their own lives at risk, to save a loved one. Self-sacrifice was the cornerstone of a genuine commitment between two people, which explained why married men and women who always put their individual selfish interests first always had the most miserable marriages. His own parents, particularly his father, had been that way, and their family had suffered as a consequence.

Winona mumbled something and pressed her face to

his neck. Nate smiled, kissed the crown of her head, and closed his eyes. If all went well they would be back at Gaona's place within two days. He could hardly wait to see Zach, Shakespeare, and Blue Water Woman again. Provided, of course, they were all still alive.

Before dawn Nate was up and saddling Pegasus. He'd had to tie the Apache horse to prevent it from running off during the night, and now the animal acted up, balking when he led it to Winona and shying away when she tried to mount. Afraid it might try to throw her, he climbed on to see if it would buck. The animal looked back at him as if wishing it could toss him clear to the moon, but it gave him no further trouble. Satisfied that it was safe for her to use, he slid down and let Winona climb up. Then he stepped to Pegasus and did the same.

This day was cooler and they made good time. At midday they stopped in a tract of woodland to rest for half an hour. Not until mid-afternoon did they come on a spring, where once again they stopped to give their horses a breather.

Nate took a chance and shot a rabbit that evening for their supper. While Winona skinned and butchered it, he prowled around their camp, satisfying himself there were no Apaches anywhere in their vicinity. The aroma from the stew Winona was preparing, which would be his first real meal in days, made his mouth water and his stomach growl like a riled wolverine.

He ate with relish, savoring every sip, slowly chewing every morsel. Halfway through he saw Winona watching him in amusement. "It's been a while," he said.

"It has," she agreed.

Nate noticed she had hardly touched her stew and mentioned as much.

"I was not talking about food, husband."

"Oh."

The smile he wore the next morning rivaled the sun for brightness. This time the Apache horse was as gentle as a lamb. Toward ten in the morning, as they came to the top of a bench, he spied a thin column of smoke in the distance.

"More Apaches?" Winona wondered.

"Let's go see," Nate proposed.

From a rise they looked down on a tranquil scene. Three small wagons laden with bags of grain were parked under trees at the side of a rutted track. Four men dressed in the white shirts and pants of New Mexican farmers were lounging in the shade while two others worked at repairing a broken wheel.

All six stood and turned as Nate and Winona approached. He reined up, glanced at the dozing oxen hooked up to the wagons, and said, *"Buenos dios."*

A lean farmer beamed and launched into a short speech in Spanish. The only phrase Nate understood was *"con mucho gusto,"* which he knew to mean "with much pleasure." He racked his brain, trying to recall the words needed to explain he couldn't speak their language worth a hoot, when Winona spoke up and in short sentences answered the farmer. The skinny man then went on again at length.

"If we follow this road it will bring us to within a mile of the Gaona *hacienda* before nightfall," she translated.

Nate saw some of the farmers were smirking at him. *"Gracias,"* he said, and wheeled Pegasus. A few of them nodded and waved.

"Is something wrong?" Winona asked as they departed.

"No."

"Then why do you look as if you just swallowed a toad?"

"Sometimes I just can't understand why a brilliant woman like you married a dunderhead like me."

"I took pity on you," Winona joked, and laughed heartily.

True to the farmer's prediction, twilight bathed the countryside when they came into sight of the familiar buildings. Immediately they broke into a gallop. Several *vaqueros* were tending stock nearby, and while two of the hands came to meet them the third raced like the wind for the *hacienda*.

By the time Nate reined up in front of the house, Francisco and his family and Shakespeare and Blue Water Woman were all there, waiting. McNair wore clean bandages that evinced a professional touch. He grinned in delight and remarked, "About time you two got back. We were beginning to think you'd decided to pay Mexico City a visit."

Nate swung down and shook his mentor's hand. Then he looked around and asked, "Where's Zach?" The faces of all there clouded and Nate felt his pulse quicken. "Where's Zach?" he repeated urgently.

Francisco was the one who answered. "I am sorry, *señor*. It is all my fault."

"What is?" Winona inquired anxiously, her hand slipping into Nate's.

"Whoa there," Shakespeare said. "It's not what you think. You'll find your young'un out back under that tall tree with the fork at the top. We figured you'd want the honor of letting him know you're back safe and sound."

Without another word Nate hurried around the house, Winona at his side. They both stopped on seeing Zach on his knees next to a mound of recently dug earth.

"Oh, no," Winona whispered.

Nate bowed his head for a moment, then advanced quietly. They were close enough to touch their son before Zach heard their footsteps and turned.

"Pa! Ma!" the boy cried, and threw himself into their arms. He broke into racking sobs, his small frame trembling, and clung to them as if his life depended on it.

"We're sorry," Nate said. "So sorry."

Zach lifted his anguished, tear-streaked face. "Why, Pa? Why did it have to happen?"

"These sort of things don't *have* to happen. They just do."

"They shot him full of arrows, Pa. Shakespeare pulled out eleven." Zach sniffed and stared forlornly at the grave. "I found him back in a ravine. From the sign, Shakespeare thinks he killed two or three of them before they got him."

"He was a scrapper," Nate said huskily.

"Francisco dug the grave himself. Said it was all his doing because he didn't have enough men on guard when the Apaches attacked us."

"No one is to blame," Nate declared.

Winona tenderly put her hand on Zach's head. "If you want, my son, we will find you a new dog after we return home. I have a cousin who would be willing to give us one."

"No, Ma."

"It might—"

"No."

Nate stepped to the mound, sank to one knee, and picked up a handful of dirt. He let the loose earth run through his fingers, thinking of the many times the mongrel had come to their aid when they were in trouble. "So long, old friend," he said.

"It ain't fair, Pa," Zach said. "It just ain't fair."

"That's the way life is," Nate responded, rising. "Sometimes things work out the way we'd like and sometimes they don't. When the worst happens, you just square your shoulders and go on living the best way you know how."

Zach's forehead creased and he glanced skyward. "Do

dogs go to heaven like people do when they die, Pa? When I get up there will I see him again?''

"I can't rightly say, son," Nate said, and added quickly when tears filled Zach's eyes, "but if ever a dog deserved it, Samson was the one. You might see him again at that.''

"I hope so, Pa. I truly hope so.''